publisher ODDNESS
artwork: MIKE DUBISCH
editor: CODY GOODFELLOW

FORBIDDEN FUTURES 6 ISBN: 9781960213211 (v2.1):

FORBIDDEN FUTURES is a trademark of ODDNESS. © 2020 USA. All rights reserved. Nothing may be reprinted in part or whole without permission from the publisher and creator. Any similarity to real people and places in fiction and semi-fiction is purely coincidental. All material in this issue is copyright to the respective creators. The publisher assumes no responsibility for unsolicited material. Printed in the USA.

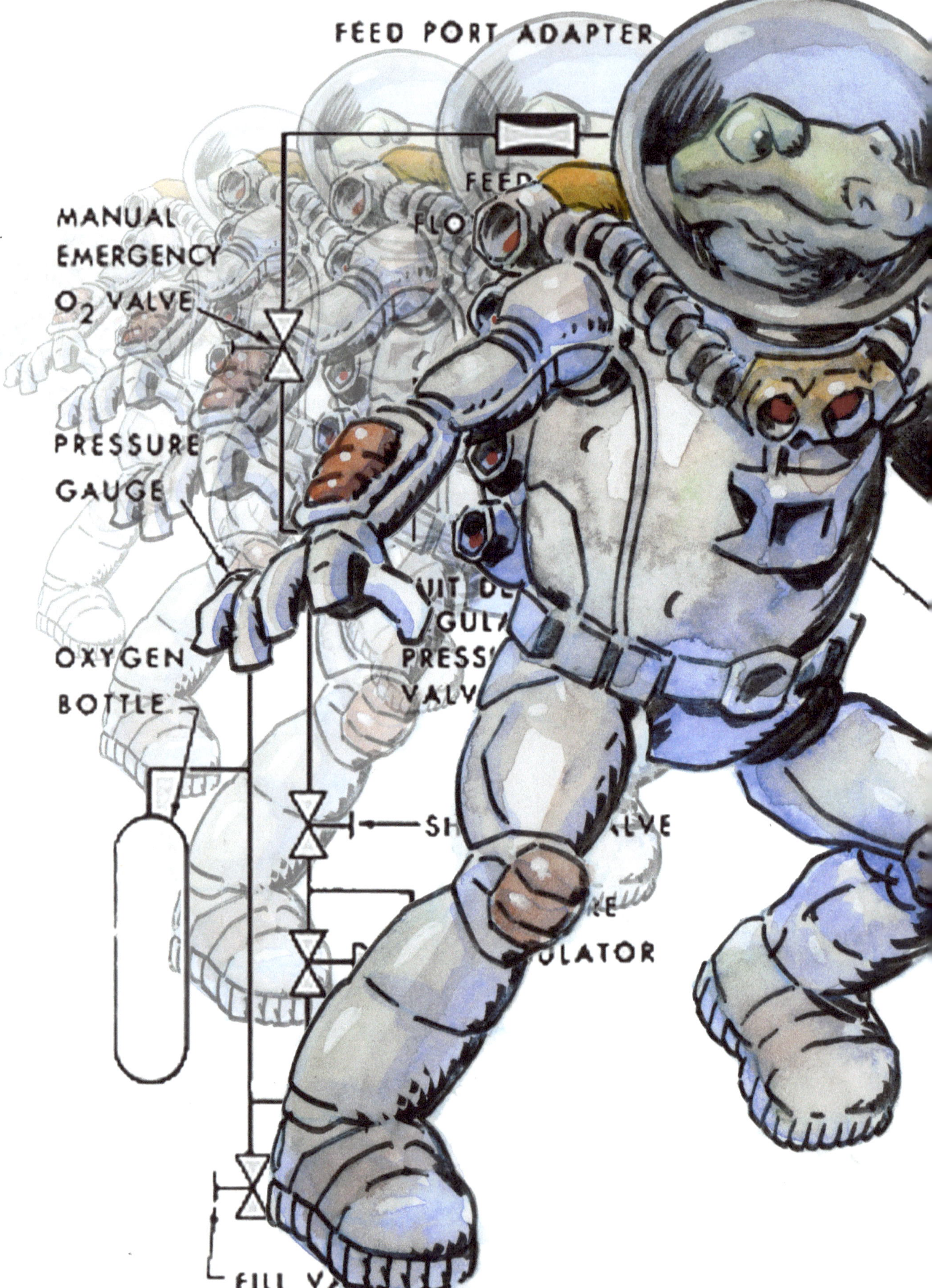
FEED PORT ADAPTER
MANUAL EMERGENCY O2 VALVE
FEED
FLO
PRESSURE GAUGE
OXYGEN BOTTLE
UIT DE
GULA
PRESS
VALV
SH   LVE
RE
ULATOR
FILL VA

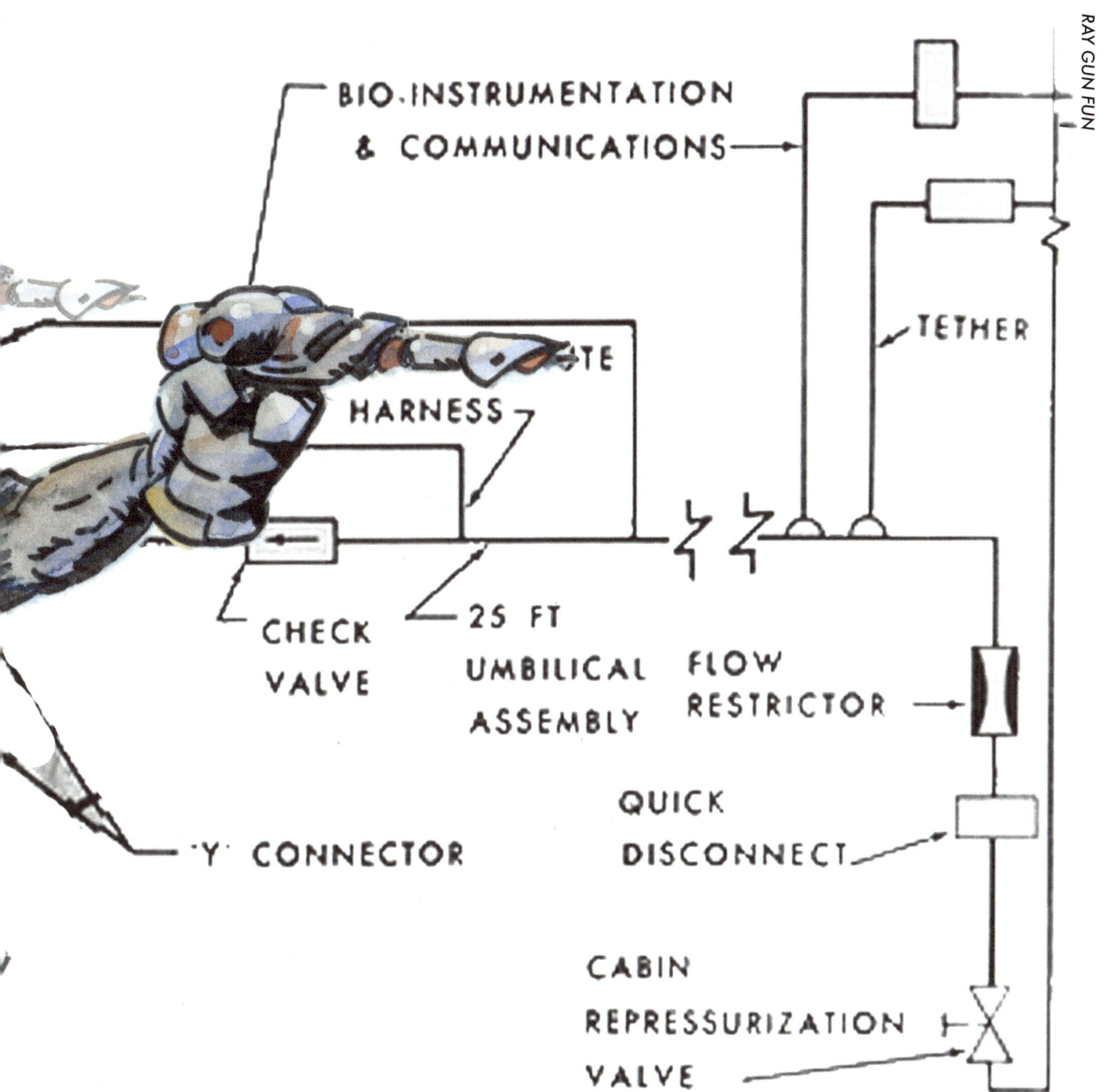

THE GERNSBACK REFERENDUM:
SEND MORE SPACE OPERA

There's a persistent bit of Hollywood apocrypha about how Stanley Kubrick included a replica of the *Discovery* spacecraft from *2001: A Space Odyssey* amid the burning rubble in the concluding scene of *Full Metal Jacket*. I've never spotted it myself despite repeated attempts, and I've failed to corroborate the legend, which I recall reading in a published edition of the screenplay, but whether it was even a real rumor or just some critic's conceit, such an objective correlative would only make literal something palpably conveyed in the rest of the film.

Somewhere in the mid-century, we lost the raygun, jet-pack future that was our birthright, even as science fiction lost a power it once exerted over every aspect of American life, a certainty that flying cars, orbital cities and interplanetary adventures were our manifest destiny.

Way back in 1981, just as he was gearing up to tear down everything that came before, William Gibson called it. In "The Gernsback Continuum," a story that was itself an anachronism next to his street-lethal cyberpunk yarns, he evoked the utopian visions of the 1930's as a dymaxion phantom haunting the modern world with tantalizing glimpses of all the future's failed fantasies. And while those visions were as threatening as they were uplifting, they haunt him as a broken promise.

I grew up in the shadow of that post-utopian hangover. The 70's were a period of ferment and self-doubt for space opera that tested Sturgeon's Law to destruction, with the genre retreating into "hard" sf math-stravaganzas, solemn predictions about the future and a lot of warmed-over Flash Gordon nostalgia. Occasional gems like Adams' *Hitchhiker's Guide* series, Spinrad's *The Iron Dream* or Harrison's *Bill The Galactic Hero* injected subversive satire into the solipsistic positivism of classic space opera, but offered no way forward. The New Wave advanced by Ellison, Dick, Farmer and others had upended the problematic hogwash of Heinlein, Campbell and Hubbard in the 60's, but like the larger cultural revolution, it only left us insecure, uncertain if we deserved a future at all.

BUT THAT PERIOD OF PESSIMISTIC BURNOUT YIELDED DIRTY GOLD, IF YOU KNEW WHERE TO LOOK: COMICS LIKE HEAVY METAL, EPIC ILLUSTRATED, EERIE, ALIEN WORLDS AND 2000 A.D., RPG'S LIKE GAMMA WORLD, TRAVELLER, STAR FRONTIERS AND CAR WARS, B-MOVIE REVELATIONS LIKE BARBARELLA, DARK STAR, THX-1138 AND ALIEN AND SIMPLER, SLEAZIER DELIGHTS LIKE STAR CRASH, FLESH GORDON, LASERBLAST, GALAXINA AND GALAXY OF TERROR.

We all watched *Star Trek* and *Twilight Zone* reruns, but for me, a newer show just felt more like life in the 1970's than anything else on TV. *Space: 1999* followed Moonbase Alpha as it hurtled on a runaway moon through space envisioned as an endless chamber of horrors. TV back then did SF on the cheap, and mostly for kids.

Yes, in its heyday, pulp sf was just another sandbox in the white male playground of pulp, offering new arenas for cleft-chinned, honky ramrods to demonstrate their superiority over green savages and alluring space-vixens alike. It may have made a hash of the science, but it inspired working people and kids to think about the future as something that could be shaped by our unfulfilled desires. Dreams rendered impossible by even basic scientific literacy were just bigger dreams.

We fully comprehend that tastes change and evolve, and many of those who welcomed the gritty cyberpunk dystopias and *Mad Max* knockoffs are the same ones fretting that they never got their flying car or a vacation on the moon today. But we lost something worth saving, if not imitating.

It would be disingenuous to lament the passing of pulp space opera, when tributes to the rocket opera serials of yesteryear so thoroughly rule our imaginations, today. But looking at the two biggest influences on modern science fiction in mainstream pop culture should give us a fix on why so much of what passes for modern space opera continues to be greasy kid stuff.

Star Wars boldly reimagined space adventure to become a ubiquitous cultural staple with its first cinematic trilogy and armadas of tie-in novels, games and TV shows, but its creators retreated from engaging with criticism by saying it was made *for* kids. While the first wave of *Star Wars* fandom captivated young and old alike, a sense persists that this is childish destiny porn that fudges the complexities of human nature as blithely as it screws up the physics, even if it's also inspired thousands of hardcore fans to discover their inner essential selves by cosplaying as tupperware-clad space Nazis.

Star Trek, likewise, offered a utopian vision of space adventure, but its successive incarnations have scrubbed away most of what makes humans recognizably human.

Its idealized Starfleet crews are weird mutants that have evolved beyond religion, capitalism and any ideology beyond the prime directive. Who are these alleged people, and how did we become them? The show never says.

CAN UNAPOLOGETICALLY FUN SCIENCE FICTION THAT'S INARGUABLY FOR ADULTS FIND A FOOTHOLD? OF COURSE IT CAN. NEW TV SERIES EVERY DAY PROVE THAT SCIENCE FANTASY THAT TREATS ADULTS LIKE ADULTS CAN THRIVE (EVEN IF HOLLYWOOD CAN'T SEEM TO MAKE BIG-BUDGET SF FILMS AT THE MOMENT, WITHOUT RELYING ON AND WRECKING MAJOR RECOGNIZED FRANCHISE BRANDS, FOR TOO MANY REASONS TO LIST HERE), AND BOTH MAINSTREAM AND INDIE PUBLISHING ARE GUSHING NEW TAKES ON SCIENCE FICTION THAT BRING BACK VINTAGE THRILLS RETROFITTED WITH MATURE THEMES, DIVERSITY AWARENESS AND AT LEAST A FRISSON OF SCIENTIFIC LITERACY. IF YOU FOLLOW IMAGE AND IDW AND THE REVAMPED HEAVY METAL, THERE'S EVEN SOME DAMNED FINE SCIENCE FICTION COMICS, AGAIN.

But ours are louder.

We hope, with this issue, to reclaim the classic tropes of bygone rocket opera as everyone's playground, and to subvert the hell out of them while rekindling a visceral hunger, if not hope, for the future. We realize Hugo Gernsback and John W. Campbell would probably be disgusted, but even if you apply Sturgeon's Law to this issue, we think you'll still have gotten your money's worth.

UNKLE KRUST'S GUIDE TO HEROES & VILLAINS OF THE SPACEWAYS

9♦ — PLANET-EATER

- —Immortal, invincible, ancient star-roving demigod; wears a mask.
- —Sees all, knows all; still can't recruit loyal herald.
- —Recycling resolution: For every planet devoured, he plants a tree at one of his golf resorts.
- —Secret weakness: can't digest planet with large deposits of Arby's franchises.

Q♣ — WASTELANDER

- —Communicates fluently with all alien fauna, but speaks English at third-grade level.
- —Lives semi-feral existence in harmony with alien ecology, but still shaves arm pits.
- —Trained in the arts of seduction by the Mantis-People of Gygax IX.
- —Secret weakness: Vogon love poetry.

J♥ — SPACE DEVIL

- —Unspeakable embodiment of cosmic evil; still wears wrestling trunks.
- —Secretly hates heavy metal.
- —Tempts you with holograms, leaves you with engrams.
- —Safe word: Xenu.

8♦   CYBORG GOONS

- Cyber-augmented clones of frequent sperm bank donor Jeffrey Epstein.
- Spines surgically enhanced so you can see their butts and breasts at the same time.
- Universal translator converts all alien languages to dubsteb wubs.
- Can repair all damage with spare parts from Radio Shack, Straight Pride rallies.

2♥   ASS-KICK CHICK

- Kicks 200% of the ass for 20% less pay.
- Sworn to overthrow galactic patriarchy; still defends Joss Whedon.
- Derives superpowers from vaping black cherry blunt atmosphere of long-lost homeworld.
- Safe word: "Mary Sue."

7♣   SPACE JERKS

- Can't read or write, but developed faster-than-light travel to cross universe, steal your water, girlfriend.
- Will trade own mother for a dime bag of Plutonian Nyborg.
- Lurks in cantinas on backwater worlds to ruin karaoke night by endlessly singing "Muskrat Love."
- Sexually dimorphic AF; they're actually screwing in this picture.

A♠   LOST ASTRONAUT

- Death sentence in three systems; STD's named after him in five.
- Causes supercomputers to melt down by explaining to them the nature of love; divorced five times.
- Can fold space by snorting Spice; can't fold own laundry.
- Trapped in time loop paradox where he periodically has to go back 1,000,000 years to create Homo sapiens with a baboon named Eve, or none of us will ever have existed. Cut him some fucking slack...

SO YOU THINK YOU CAN LIVE?
BY LUCIO RODRIGUEZ

Bibi stumbled to the couch, blue-synth flower print, the cushions almost up to her head. She climbed up with her bowl of grapes, immediately started putting on a chest plate connected to a bulbous laser gun. The chest plate reads, "Valkyrie brand auto-synchronizing participatory vest with viewer-voting laser," words Bibi can't read, but the commercial repeated often enough that she was able to ask her mother to order it.

Her chubby, late-toddler fingers pressed the channel button until the VTV-8 logo appeared on the large flat screen. Bibi wriggled with excitement.

The voiceover begins, "For decades, Valkyrie has been your go-to for food, streaming entertainment, books, bio-modification, and same-day delivery for products across the world." The screen scrolls through images of produce, libraries, scientists walking a dog-sized elephant.

"We wanted more. We wanted…Mars." Images of rockets, terraformers, scientists examining plants and seeds.

"Well, we goofed…" The image changes to terraformers malfunctioning, spewing tainted gasses and liquids over red soil. When the smoke clears, there's all manner of aberrant creatures skittering away. A snake-like dragon swims through the air, soars toward a rocky red mountain; the camera swoops past, reaches the peak, covered in gold coins and bones and gems. Atop this a green flag waves, bearing a prominent Valkyrie 'V'.

"But now our mistake is your favorite reality show! We've dropped twenty contestants across Mars. Their goal? Survive."

Bibi stands on the couch, mimes the huge guitar riff that comes from the television; her vest vibrates in time, LEDs scroll up and down. Upbeat music fills the room, and the screen explodes with the show's logo, "So You Think You Can Live?"

"Bibi, don't stand on the couch," mom calls from the other room, the apathy of daily occurrence.

Above Edita's head, the first of five green bulbs came to life. The color was garish, too much for her eyes, now two weeks accustomed to the red soil and sky outside.

The show was about to start. In five minutes, her bunker would blossom open. Already two contestants had been lost at bunker-open. One overslept and never woke. Carbon monoxide poisoning. The other contestant, Phil, had made the highlight reels.

A flat screen occupied one wall of her bunker. This was how Valkyrie gave them updates, rule changes, and carefully redacted highlights from previous episodes.

It was on that screen that she'd seen Phil's final moments. He had made two fatal mistakes; first, he led the rathounds to the bunker he holed up in, and second, a last-minute bathroom break. The scene of him flailing the undonned portions of his crustacean-like suit had already been remixed and set to the Benny Hill theme.

The fizzle of the final bulb igniting. Edita was near top speed, launched herself from a still-falling wall. Gravity here was a third what it was on Earth, which afforded her several seconds of air-time.

Tracks on the ground, rathounds probably, based on the size and number. They were pack hunters— the dumbest and hungriest pack hunters. Edita would know, she had been part of Valkyrie's Mars habituation/population project.

Edita landed. No immediate threats. She checked her compass for the next bunker zone. Up ahead, a forest, and before that a single rathound using the side of its jaw to gnaw at a boulder.

So dumb.

Probably best to be on her way, but… She drew her laser pistol—it was something out of Flash Gordon, copper colored, a series of spheres that shrank in size and ended in a wire-frame reticle.

She sighed.

Now was as good a time as any to find out what today's surprise would be.

"Make your selection!"

Bibi's vest came to life, LED's running along shell-like crests toward her right hand. They ran along her arm, the fins accentuating the arrow affect. On a small screen on her pistol, four options appeared.

On-screen the choices were tallied, converted to percentages, and a pie chart was adjusted to reflect those percentages. Bibi was excited to see that her choice occupied half the now-spinning pie chart.

//

The dial on the laser pistol spun. Rathound in her sights, she waited. The dial stopped on "pew."

"Pew? What the balls is—"

The pistol began quaking in her hand, energy coalescing at its tip. Edita put both hands around the grip, braced her stance.

When Edita saw the word, "pew," she assumed a tiny, probably useless shot. She expected a really dumb noise, not unlike the swap meet toys that cycled through the same eight sounds. From her experience so far, neither of these were unlikely.

Instead, an enormous bolt of energy ripped from the tip of her pistol, throwing Edita onto her back. The shot splattered the rathound and destroyed half the boulder.

Also, the gun went *PEW*, a roaring, throaty man's voice.

Edita got to her feet, patted red dust from herself. "Well, I was half right."

She checked her suit. Oxygen lines seemed fine, and the crests and ridges that ran along the armored suit—the ones she had mocked on first sight—bore the brunt of the damage.

Fine, but we still look like Atlantean gladiators.

She was sore in weird places. Shoulder blades. The top of her thighs. It was a reality show, after all. The producers' goal was to accentuate each contestant's assets. For a hunky guy, the camera would frame his face to catch his intense blue eyes, or linger on his pecs, enhanced by generously shaped armor. For the ladies, well, it was boobs and butts, and camera angles that were either voyeuristic or overly familiar. As a result, Edita's suit didn't quite—

The sound of pistol fire nearby, semi-auto, coming down the hillside and through the trees.

Ahead of her.

Dammit.

She headed to the tree line at a jog, the low gravity extending her stride. More gunfire. Close, but the tangled trees made it difficult to see farther than a few meters.

If she could, Edita would like to skirt past this gunfire. She didn't want to meet either the contestant or whatever they were facing.

The gunfire died. Someone had claimed a victory.

She didn't even have time for a sigh of relief. A deafening snap, and a tree was felled in her path. A monster emerged.

It was a crab. Mostly. Without the constraints of gravity or ethics, it was the size of a large car that had eaten a larger car. Parts of it were misshapen, plates disjointed, like its body was fighting itself to stay together.

Edita's wristcom chimed. An image of the creature appeared; from the right "Megacrab" slammed into frame.

"No," Edita called out, trying to find the drone that was filming her. "That's a stupid name. I'm not calling it that."

The megacrab hammered another tree with the larger of its claws. The roots tore, black sap pulsing from them. It hoisted the felled tree, jerked it back and forth in that uneven crab manner. Edita sidestepped the initial swing, was caught in a jerky backhand. Branches scraped at her armor and helmet, leaves the thickness of fruit-leather rasped her face.

The megacrab skittered to one side, then the other when Edita feinted. Dust kicked up in both directions.

Good, she thought, *it makes up for being gigantic by being really fast.*

She pulled her pistol. No knowing how hard that chitin was, and the noise was bound to attract attention, but there was no avoiding it.

Carmela walked into frame, skin tight dress the rusty red of Martian sand. She faced the camera, Juan-Carlos in the background over her shoulder. She was on the verge of tears.

Juan-Carlos reached out, but his feet wouldn't move. "Carmela—"

"No! No puedes bailar!"

//

"Mommy! Jay is changing the channel!" Bibi reached over, grasped for the controller in her brother's hand.

"No, I didn't," Jay called out. "She sat on it."

From the other room, "If you two are going to fight over the television, I'm just going to throw it in the trash! Jay, you know it's time for your sister's show. Leave her alone!"

"Fine, I've got homework to do, anyway." He tossed the controller at the couch.

Bibi waited until her brother had left the room, then stuck out her tongue.

//

The megacrab lay upside down, its remaining legs twitching in spastic strokes. A drone lay embedded into its left side, on fire, and a tree lay across everything, also on fire.

Edita allowed herself to drop onto her butt with a sigh. She rolled awkwardly, trying to find a comfortable way to sit.

That. *That,* had been the shot of a lifetime. If that shot hadn't ricocheted the way it did...

Her wristcom pinged. She looked at it, a message from the producers—*seriously? In its claw?*

She wandered around the megacrab debris, found its claw, retrieved a small package. She eyed her defeated foe. Legs in the background, that was the shot. A couple taps on her 'com and a drone flew in low, hovered around head-height.

Edita dipped her hip, smiled, held the unwrapped package near her face.

"Nothing gets between me and my 300% Ultra-condensed butter!"

A couple poses for ad shots—winking; Blue Steel; kissing the package.

///

"Mo-m! We need new butter!"

///

Edita's wristcom pinged again. *So soon?* She glanced down, nodded. The bunker zone was in range.

A short jog and a leap across a five-meter canyon, she found herself looking down a craggy cliff face onto the bunker zone. A ring of five bunkers.

Five contestants lost in the last 48 hours.

And if the producers wanted a big climax for the last few episodes, they were going to be disappointed. Below her, a contestant was locking down all the bunkers, hitting their occupancy button and exiting before it sealed up for the night.

Edita had to get down there, had to get into one of those bunkers. You didn't want to be out at night on Mars.

She descended quickly, low gravity her friend. First bunker, locked. Second, third, the same. The man she had seen earlier filled the doorway of the fourth. He was big, would probably seem big even without the armored suit.

"I'm sorry, no vacancies. Unless you wish to join Marco for the night."

He rolled the R in his name. Gross.

"Get out. I'm taking that bunker." Edita put her hand on her pistol.

"Do not be a fool, Marco also has a gun." He hit the lockdown button. The five second countdown started.

"Not like this one."

Marco's eyes widened. The laser pistol whined, the pitch getting so high it ascended into inaudibility. Edita watched Marco gauge his options.

He leaped from the door.

PEW.

The bunker rocked back, teetered on its back edge before falling forward again, its front face shredded. A single beat, and the remaining walls fell.

Edita was lying on the ground several meters away. Marco appeared over her, furious.

"What have you done?"

Edita turned her pistol to Marco. He reached for his pistol, realized he'd lost it somewhere. He raised his hands.

"We're going to die out here! Marco is displeased."

Edita's gun didn't waiver. "We're in a reality show about trying to survive on an inhospitable planet that we've made more inhospitable. We were probably going to die anyway."

"You've doomed us all. We're not going to survive the night."

"No, we're good. I only destroyed one bunker. We can just use one of the other—oh, no. You already locked down all the other ones!"

A stand-off. Marco would have to be dumber than the rathounds to let her stand up. Her arms were getting tired, holding this position; she adjusted her grip, she saw the info panel on the side. It read, "Pew Ammo: 1/3."

That wasn't good.

From beyond the edge of the bunkers, more voices.

"Marco is over here! He is held at gunpoint!"

"I, wait, no!"

Two men and a woman came into view.

///

The woman moved in slow motion, her name slamming onto the screen. "Karen." To the side were her stats, which Bibi never could make sense of. Instead, she liked to look at their favorite foods: Kroger brand mashed potatoes, corn dogs. Owned two cats. Wrestling, which was a hard word to read, and harder still, Bibi sounded out, "Tak-ti-tile...dis-a-door?"

The camera had to zoom out to get the tall man completely in frame. "Laslow." It said he had over seven feet, though Bibi could only count two. Oprah brand bread, and I Can't Believe it's Not Soy-milk.

The other man started his slow-mo walk, "Ricardo" slammed onto the screen, but Bibi was distracted. Jay sat on the couch near her. No, he sat on the couch, but near *the remote.* In that sibling rivalry sixth sense, she knew he was closer to the remote than she was, and he was *thinking* about touching it.

///

"The crap?" Karen asked. "Why are all these locked?"

Marco pointed at Edita. "She did it—"

"I did not!" Edita protested.

"—and then she blew up that one. Marco tried to stop her."

"Okay, that's true—"

"Why the hell—we're going to die out here!"

"Look, I already had that conversation with Ricardo Montelban over here—"

"My great-grandfather?" the shorter man asked.

"—the show is literally called, 'So You Think—Wait. Are you really related to Ricardo Montelban?"

"Ricardo Montelban the Fourth." He bowed, smiled. She saw it, it was the dimples.

Karen drew her pistol. Edita pointed her own at the woman, then back at Marco, who nearly pounced in that split second.

The tall man, Laslow, asked languidly, "Well, now what?"

"Well," Karen said. "She's doomed us. If all I get is to live longer than she does, I'll take it."

"'s kind of a bummer, but in for a penny." Laslow pointed his gun.

One shot left.

She kicked off the ground at an angle and fired a moment later, aiming her shot at the ground between herself and the others. The shot blasted dust into the air, obscuring everyone and everything; their hard-light shots peppered the sand where she had been laying.

"Bloody feces," Karen coughed out. "What the hell was that!"

The shot threw Edita some fifteen meters. She landed in a three-point stance, scrambled into a sprint.

The terrain here was rough and uneven, with tall rock protrusions. She was constantly having to switch back along her path, but on the plus side—half a dozen bullets struck a protrusion—*that.*

Away. Just get away. She leaped a crevasse, crested a dune, and looked down on her old workplace…

A mirage, Edita thought, seeing the massive facility. Large forklift drones moved shipping containers from the facility to the yard, and smaller drones whizzed through the air.

Edita slapped her forehead. Of course Valkyrie had a distribution center here! How else were the bunkers being delivered? The same-day supply drops? Who was strapping butter to monsters?

It was an exact replica of the one Edita had worked in. Shipping here, receiving over there. Probably a lab and production in the basement level.

Inside, person-sized drones moved packages to and fro; they auto-piloted out of her way while she walked the central path. Above, secondary and tertiary floors of heavy scaffolding. She climbed,

hoping it was just one more obstacle between her and—

Shots exploded around her, projectiles sparking off metal railing.

///

Bibi gripped the couch, chubby knuckles turning white. On the screen, Edita dove, crawled between some cases. Karen, a level below, shoved through several carrier drones. Two more short bursts, which struck the side nearest Edita.

Edita seemed lost. She drew her pistol, shook her head. She ran away from Karen and climbed the stairs to the third level.

"No, there's more that way! Turn around!"

The camera shifted to Marco and Laslow taking position behind a support column. Marco, still gunless, caught Edita in the ribs with a 2x4; she staggered back.

Laslow stepped out, pistol drawn, less than two meters from Edita.

Bibi gripped her pistol, aimed with all her might at the television.

"Make your selection!" her chest plate sounded.

She forgot, for a moment, the drama on the screen. Among the new choices was her favorite thing in the world.

///

Laslow was tall, lanky. His hand covered most of the pistol's grip and body, so he didn't notice that the dial had begun spinning. Whatever it was, Edita was certain her time was up.

"I'm sorry, man," Laslow droned. "It's just the game."

The dial slowed, stopped.

Laslow pulled the trigger. Thousands of bubbles erupted from the nose of his gun.

///

"Bubbles!" Bibi bounced on the couch.

///

Edita pulled back, punched Laslow in the gut.

"Yeah, I deserved that," he groaned.

"You are worthless." Marco grabbed Laslow, leveraged his forearm and tossed him over the rail.

Laslow fell several levels to the floor. He lay there, called up, "Messed up, man."

Marco's face snapped to Edita. "You!" he roared. He was on her instantly, grabbed at her waist and shoulder. Edita grasped his arms, attempted to pry his hands away. He was too strong. She was over his head; Marco spun her and hurled her over the rail.

Edita shrieked.

She shrieked again, and her enthusiasm waned.

Marco was strong, too strong for Mars' gravity. The air-time was somewhere around fifteen seconds. She landed a level down in a coordinations hub, skidded across a table and landed amongst computers and chairs. She grabbed the table beside her to lift herself up, her hand slipping on a keyboard.

The screen read, "Mnjko;ioikpj not found."

Edita looked at the screen, the keyboard. She typed furiously, smiling as each item she checked came up as "in stock," and, "same day delivery."

A table flipped over a railing. Karen. With a single hand she gripped another table, flipped it, too, over the rails on the opposite side.

Karen squared up, keeping her body low. Her hands shot out occasionally, grasping for Edita's arms and head; Edita leaped back, bumped into a table.

Karen clearly had combat training. Edita was worried. A fist-fight was one thing, but crap went out the window when someone started with cartwheel-kicks or hadokens or whatever.

Edita grabbed the keyboard. Karen guarded like she expected a swing, but Edita furiously typed a single word and clicked "Enter."

A drone zoomed overhead, paused, dropped a tub of Nope, It's Still Not Butter into Edita's hands.

"Primo delivery," Edita smiled.

"The crap is that supposed to do?" Karen snarled. She tried to close distance with Edita.

Edita deftly unwrapped the butter and, still circling, slathered it on her arms and legs.

Karen shot in, so fast Edita realized the previous attempts had been a ploy. Karen grabbed high on Edita's arm, shifted her weight in a move that should have slammed Edita to the ground. Instead Karen's hands slid off forcefully.

"The fu—this is nasty!" Karen flapped and flicked her hand, trying to dislodge the butter. "Why would—? This is—" She was visibly upset. "Ugh! Okay, please, please. I don't want to kill you anymore. Just," she swatted her hand against the table, against the railing, "get me something to wipe this off with!"

Seconds later a roll of paper towels fell into Karen's hands. She struggled with the packaging. Her wristcom pinged. "What, you've got to be—ugh! Fine!" She faced a nearby drone, held the paper towels aloft, and declared, "You don't have to surrender to filth when you use Calico Lumberjack's infinite-absorbent paper towels!"

//

"This show is dumb. It's all commercials," Jay said.

"It's not dumb. You're dumb."

"Ugh, whatever. It's been over an hour. It's my turn."

Jay reached for the controller.

Bibi leaped.

//

Marco dropped onto the platform, 2x4 still in hand. He swung, clearing a desk; papers exploded everywhere. Edita scrambled back, pounded away at the keyboard.

He swung again, a glancing strike, but caught her full on the backswing. Marco doubled up, catching her again, low and solid; the strike threw her into a monitor.

Edita stood quickly, surprised how little that last hit hurt. She turned, looking over her shoulder. The exaggerated left butt-cheek of her suit was shattered.

"You broke my ass!" she shouted. She slammed her index finger on the Enter key.

Behind Marco a cage dropped onto the platform. The doors swung open, and a dozen frenzied rathounds emerged.

Marco looked at the rathounds, back at Edita.

Edita smiled, raised the keyboard to eye level, plucked the Enter key.

Behind her a bunker dropped onto the scaffolding. She stepped back, waved, then slammed the lockdown button.

//

"Fine, fine!" Jay screamed. He dropped the controller, tried to roll away.

Bibi rose, triumphant. She looked down at her brother, spit a tooth onto the floor beside him. Her first loose tooth!

She looked up in time to see Edita collapse on the floor of her bunker, smiling.

"Coming up next," the television announced, "Planet Kardasian!"

Bibi pooched out her lips in thought. "Umm. No."

Click.

"HE BLEW HIS LOAD"
BY MAX BOOTH III

We were drunk as fuck on some planet with far too many consonants and not nearly enough vowels in its name. After a while, they all start blurring together. Only difference between all these planets is sometimes the primary species has tails. And sometimes the air will melt your flesh, but this wasn't one of those planets.

One common trend throughout the galaxy, though? Booze. Inevitably, some entrepreneur will be peddling something guaranteed to rewire your brain.

I hid in the corner of ZYXXXLER'S TAVERN with a pitcher of some green radioactive beverage. Had a minty aftertaste to it. I eavesdropped on the locals gossiping politics: some official had been caught taking bribes for a new interdimensional monorail that was leaking poison into the sewers—and, rather than resign, he'd tried to disintegrate the planet's populace. I wasn't sure he'd failed.

My comlink vibrated. An S-O-S text from Jake.

I finished the pitcher before heading across the bar. The bathroom was locked, so I knocked and shouted, "Jake? Hell's going on in there?"

Some barmaid pulled me inside. The one Jake was flirting with earlier. Her skin was green and scaly, which I knew to be one of Jake's biggest fetishes. Dude loved to fuck lizard people.

Something in this bathroom must've been hilarious, because she couldn't stop laughing.

Jake shouted my name from a stall. He lay sprawled in a puddle of blood with his breeches off next to his discarded ray gun. A blackened crater where his cock used to be.

"What the fuck happened here?"

Jake pointed at his crotch. "I messed up, man."

I grabbed the barmaid by her shoulders. "What did you do to him, you witch!"

Still laughing, she shook me off. "He did that to himself."

"Did what?"

"He…" She doubled over, unable to control herself. "He shot it off."

"It was an accident." Jake moaned, writhing in his own blood. "Got impatient with my belt. And…it just went off."

"Okay." Deep breath. "Where'd it go?"

"That's the thing." He licked his lips. "It, uh… got away."

"Got away?"

Still laughing, the barmaid pointed at a drain in the floor, where a stream of Jake's blood had flowed. "It fell in the sewer!"

Tears streaming down Jake's face. "She's been making fun of me the whole time. Like it's a fuckin' joke. Oh god, what am I gonna do?"

It seemed obvious, albeit beyond fucked up. "I'm gonna fetch your cock, then we'll put it on ice and take it to the nearest clinic."

"You think they'll be able to reattach it?"

The best answer I could give him in that moment was a shrug. I kneeled in Jake's blood and tried prying open the drain, but the metal grate seemed fused to the floor. I lay flat on my stomach, not caring about getting blood on me, and pressed my eye against the grate, searching for my buddy's cock.

There was the whole package, half-submerged in sewer water.

Except, the water was green, and glowing, like the shit I'd been drinking back at my table. It fizzed and sizzled like liquid nitrogen on a hot grill…

And it was doing something to Jake's dismembered member.

Its sides started bulging…mutating…then…

…eyeballs emerged from its shriveled head…

…and teeth…

It hissed at me.

"Ahhh!" I rolled away.

"What?" Jake tried getting up, fell back down.

"Your cock's got a face."

"My what's got a what?"

I pointed at the barmaid. "What kinda shit's down there?"

She shrugged.

"Why does his cock have a face?"

Another shrug. "Things from all over the galaxy come here to drink and dump… things're bound to get interesting."

Jake started crying again. "What do you mean it has a face?"

Fuck it.

I whipped out my own ray gun and blasted the drain. The barmaid screamed. I stomped the blackened floor and the tile crumbled into the sewer. Bingo.

The dick wasn't impressed. It stared up at me, growling like a rabid slamhound, ready to bite.

I hesitated, afraid of losing my hand to this fucking monstrosity. Would Jake have given it a second thought, if our positions were reversed?

Of course not. Jake was a true friend. I couldn't let him down.

I holstered my ray gun and dropped to the floor when—

ZAP!

"Oh fuck."

I rolled on my side, both hands over my crotch as blood gushed out between my fingers

"Oh fuck oh fuck oh fuck…"

The barmaid laughed so hard, snot exploded from her face. "Oh look! They're so adorable…"

I felt around for my own member, but you know where it went.

We lay by the drain until the med-bots came for us— hearing them moving down there, whispering to each other, doing things for which no species in the galaxy has words.

Jake and I drifted apart after that and neither of us ever went back there, but I like to think by now, our cocks spawned a new species and took over that shithole planet as the new apex predators.

If you ever go there, I'd love to hear about it…

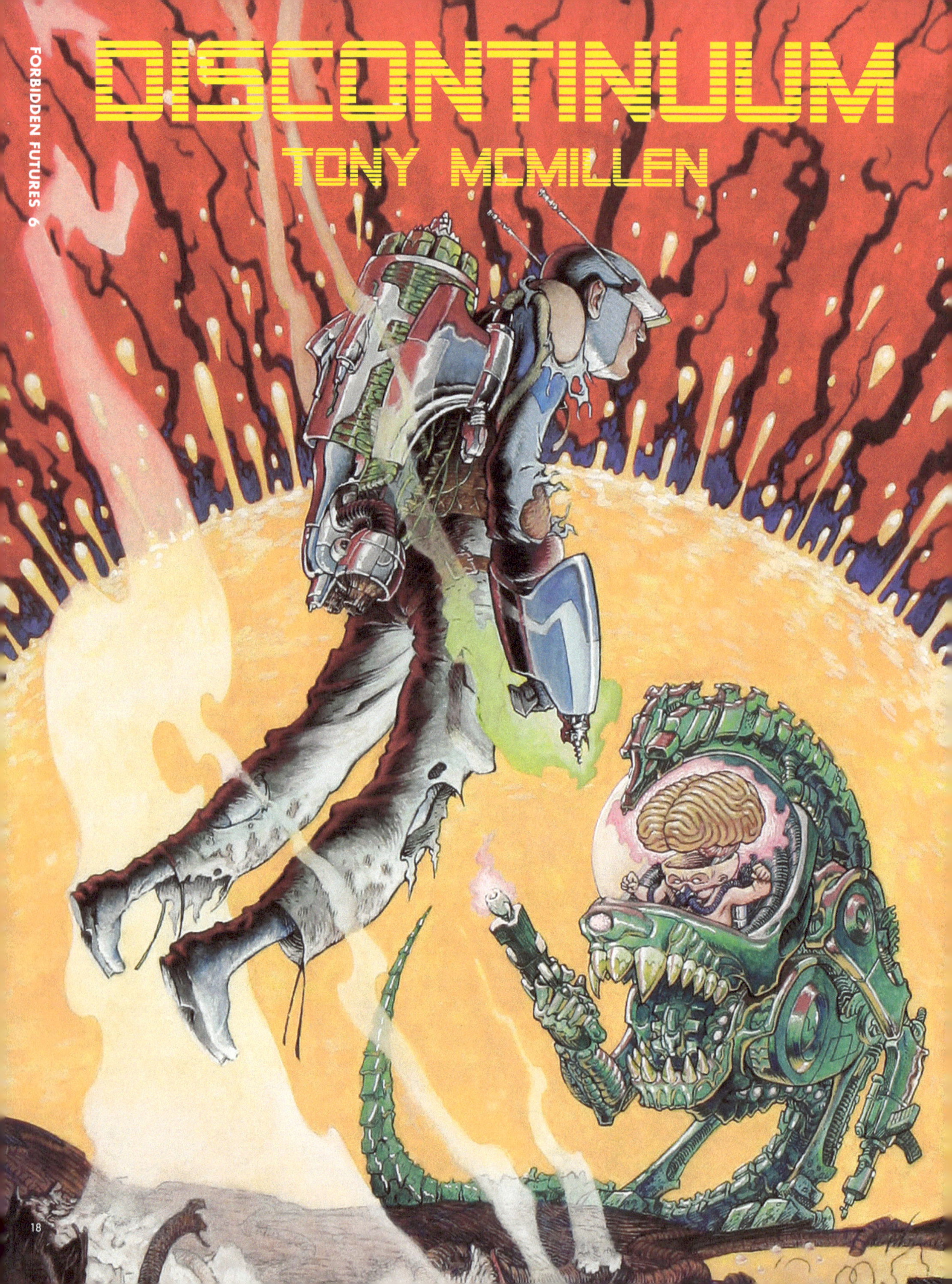

FORBIDDEN FUTURES 6
DISCONTINUUM
TONY MCMILLEN
18

We were midwives to dying stars. Coroners for corpse galaxies and homicide detectives for murdered realities. But mostly, we were just janitors for thoughts deemed too stupid or perfect to survive. I don't think any of us knew who made the big decisions, we just did what we were told. Luckily we were told very little. Today I was told to take care of the Brain-Baby. Seeing as that was its name, I could see why it had to go.

Not that there wasn't something there. Brain-Baby was a chubby cherub with an opened skull cavity above its eyes like a big empty ice cream bowl with a floating brain hovering above in a splash of pink energy. Oh, and the baby was in the cockpit of a bio-mechanical exoskeleton, replete with bony metal tail and jagged gnashing teeth. You could do something with that. But *Brain-Baby...?* I mean, *Brainchild* is just sitting there, right?

But something wouldn't be discontinued for having a bad name. *Discontinued* is what we call it when we do our job. Something with a bad name could just be given another go-over with no need for complete discontinuation. So I wondered what else was wrong with Brain-Baby? That wasn't my job – wondering – but you can't just be your job. Least I can't.

When I found my way to where the Brain-Baby was currently being staged I also spotted the little guy's chief antagonist, Hoverpack Hank. Hank used to go by the name Jetpack Jim (which I argue is a better handle), but the powers that be changed it to Hank. Not that too many care one way or the other. Hank and his soon-to-be discontinued rival Brain-Baby are both unrealized creations of some sci-fi comic strip artist's imagination. I forget his name, I'm lousy with details, but I think it's an alliteration just like his characters. Which gives me forgiveness for his naming all his characters stuff like Brain-Baby or Hoverpack Hank. He published a slew of other stuff in his time, all of it was great, but he had even more ideas like Hank and Brain-Baby stuffed away which never got published, or even drawn. Stuff that practically haunted him, but never committed to paper. For some reason even ideas that never go anywhere sometimes have to be discontinued, according to my bosses. I'll never understand why.

Take Brain-Baby, who's he hurting? Besides wanting to enslave humanity as his milk-slaves (seriously, this guy decided *not* to publish this one?) Brain-Baby is just minding his business. Harmless, no one will ever know about him. The artist dies and Brain-Baby goes with him. The only ones who ever know are me, the big bosses and my coworkers. Not that they ever want to talk about it. Or anything else much at all.

Which is why it was so strange when I saw my fellow discontinuer named Priestly waiting just beside the frozen in space Brain-Baby. Priestly wasn't his real name; we don't have real names. We are just discontinuers but I thought, what's the harm? So I told him, (not really a him but he just feels like a him) *I'm gonna call you Priestly and -if you like - call me, Nairne.* Priestly didn't seem to like or dislike this idea, he just gave me a look then left the station on to his next assignment. But now he was waving me over, an approximation of a smile on his approximation of a face.

"Hello..."

"It's Nairne, remember? See, I chose our names from history; I asked myself, if we-"

"That's the whole pickle really."

"Bad names, I know! Brain-Baby..." I made an approximation of a scoff. "And just between us, Priestly, they should have stuck with Jetpack Jim."

I thought I recognized an approximation of a wince on Priestly's face as he raised his discontinuum device and aimed it at me. "My name is not Priestly, my name is nothing, so is yours. We are meant to serve, not question, not name. ...They've decided to discontinue you."

"...Why?'

"That's why! Too many questions."

"Is this because I made you Priestly? You can be Nairne or better – you pick your own name!"

"Goodbye."

"At least say, *Goodbye, Nairne.*"

"I'm sorry. ...I can't."

He started up the device, there'd be a moment before it hummed on and I out. "One last question."

"No!"

"Is Brain-Baby not being discontinued, then?"

Approximated sound of exasperation. "No, it's being discontinued, no one will ever remember it, just like you, I'm afraid."

The hum of the device swelled. "But I won't forget."

"Yes..." Approximation of a sigh. "But you'll be gone."

"But you won't, and you'll remember it and me." The hum of the discontiuum roared. "How could you forget me?" Approximation of a shaky smile. "I'm the one who gave you a name."

THE INSUPERABLE BRUTE GIBSON

DAVID W. BARBEE

Nothing was going to bring Brute Gibson down, though the universe was damn sure trying. Fate itself started lusting for his blood on November 12, 1988, the night he was supposed to win his big match at the Georgia Dome but was transubstantiated across millions of miles of space right before walking through the curtain. First it was the civil war between the Martian moons, then defeating the hydrogen pirates on Neptune, saving the precious spice calves of Betelgeuse, and on and on, bouncing deeper into the Milky Way, bouncing off alien landscapes like a pinball, bringing chaos and adventure with every crash landing.

He'd worn shaggy loincloths in the tar swamps of Heckhole IV and sleek jumpsuits while clinging to continent-sized star cruisers. He'd impregnated alien tsarinas who still smiled at the thought of his bulging arms and beery breath. Their little bastards, with their half-sized horns or tentacles or nose ridges, felt proud to be the castoff progeny of Brute Gibson. Fourteen religions had been started in his name. There were armies worth of men he'd taught to wrestle. He'd journeyed countless lightyears, building a legend that was whispered between the stars.

So he was furious when the legend was stolen from him.

You get enemies blasting around the universe and sticking your human appendages into alien cultures. Warlords wanted Brute's head for honor or revenge or both. Mad scientists and fringe cults laid claim to all the other parts of his body.

Enter Gorilla Gruel. Chieftain of the Simianites. Interstellar pirate and interspecies terrorist. An Earthling animal abducted years ago and genetically enhanced by a crew of jaded biomongers, Gruel escaped his captors and since gathered a battalion of test monkeys to his cause. Every so often he led them on half-baked schemes to jumpstart their evolution and become something akin to homo sapiens, which GrueAl considered to be the universe's most divine creature. Gruel was particularly fascinated by Brute Gibson, interpreting his presence in the universe as a sign of the Simianites' ascendency and the subjugation of all peoples beneath the godhood of Gorilla Gruel. Usually it was easy for Brute to foil Gruel's apish agitations, but every now and then, even an interstellar superhero finds himself strapped down to an ancient surgery altar, haloed by hovering scalpels.

After the darkness, Brute awoke in Gorilla Gruel's shaggy form. The smooth pink Adonis his mother bore was long gone with that delusional monkey brain at the wheel. So went another chapter of Brute Gibson's adventures in the stars, but this time was different. It was personal. Brute went on the warpath from world to world, pursuing his enemy even as, to the rest of the universe, their roles were reversed. For Gorilla Gruel, it was his ultimate dream come true. Not only was he human, he was Brute Gibson. He went on tour, visiting the sites of all Brute's greatest adventures and reaping the rewards of celebrity. He attended every holiday in his honor, feasted and drank with his adoring fans, fucked every princess in sight, no matter how many tentacles she had.

To bring Gruel to justice, Brute needed help. Luckily, the ape had so many stars in his eyes he'd forgotten his Simianite followers. Brute simply pretended to be Gorilla Gruel and had the loyalty of those spacefaring savages.

They struck the Fourth Annual Brute Gibson Wrestlefest almost immediately.

Gorilla Gruel's mouth roared. His long black fingers worked the various triggers and buttons on his ray gun, spraying rainbow-colored death on the civilians in the crowd. The Simianites had breached the surrounding colosseums while their leader raided the central stage on his cloudskipper.

Down next to the wrestling ring, Brute Gibson's body reclined on a dais of cushions, smoking a hookah. That insane monkey, stealing the glory of Brute Gibson for himself. The gorilla's mouth roared again. As the cloudskipper dived like a meteor, Brute Gibson wondered. He was living Gorilla Gruel's life now, and maybe that was what made anybody who they were. Maybe he was the ape. Maybe the Brute Gibson down below was really Brute Gibson. Maybe there was little difference between them, two crude beings sowing chaos in the fertile fields of the final frontier.

He couldn't know it, but before the cloudskipper exploded them both, Brute Gibson wondered the same thing.

Cosmic Goblet
Rhys Hughes

WHAT A TYRANT SLUBBER WAS! HE MATERIALISED ONE DAY IN THE CRYSTAL CITY. HE TOOK OVER THE PALACE OF THE PEOPLE AND MADE IT HIS HOME. HE WAS AN INDOLENT MAN, YET HE COULD CLOBBER EVERY HERO IN THE REGION IF HE SO WISHED.

Next to his bed was a goblet into which he urinated in the middle of the night. He was too lazy to get up and relieve himself in the bathroom. The goblet was big and he never emptied it until it was full. After a year of his rule, the citizens decided to fight back.

They doubted they could kill him, so they resolved to humiliate him instead, but none dared do so. At last a young man by the name of Frapper volunteered for the task. The form the mockery would take was left up to him.

One night, Frapper entered the palace dressed in armour, an ultraglass helmet on his head. He carried a sword. Nothing would protect him if Slubber woke, so he walked on tiptoes to the side of the bed. The goblet was already full.

Carefully he picked it up and backed out of the room without disturbing the tyrant. This daring theft was an achievement in itself and Slubber had been mocked to a degree that would satisfy the citizens.

But Frapper felt it wasn't sufficient. He left the palace and went to the airlock in the side of the dome that covered the city. He passed through it onto the barren surface. The greater the distance the goblet was from Slubber, the greater the mockery.

With the goblet levitating in his antigravity glove, he set off. His resolve was firm during the journey, as the weight of the goblet decreased, for there was always some incident that occurred to make him spill a little liquid.

These incidents came in the form of interferences by solar storms, meteorite strikes, swooping space pirates, astro-beasts and other cosmic monsters. But he never lost heart, because he was aware that the humiliation of Slubber was on the increase with each league further he went.

His beard grew long inside his helmet and he peered into the goblet to check how much liquid was left. He knew that starlight was evaporating it a little every day. The level was only half now.

He reached out to touch it and something surged through him. He leapt back. The feeling of humiliation seemed to be less. He had the idea that Slubber was not quite as humiliated as he had been one day ago. As if the effect had peaked and was now weakening.

The strength of the humiliation was directly related to the distance between the liquid in the goblet and Slubber's body. Could it be that Slubber had left the city and was chasing Frapper, that he was catching up with him? He must be mounted on a hoverscooter.

Frapper pushed himself to his limit. He plunged into adventure after adventure. He battled energy worms and hibernating robots activated by the vibrations of his boots as he passed the cave mouths where they slumbered.

As he travelled in this manner he noticed something odd taking place around him. The general look of the landscape was coming back to the style he knew. And now he passed through a zone of basalt formations that resembled those of his youthful explorations.

He crested a ridge and saw a city before him.

He gasped. He recognised this city and its protective dome. This was his home. He had gone all the way around the world.

Slubber wasn't following him. That wasn't the reason for the decline in the sensation of humiliation that emanated from the goblet. Nor was the decline in any way connected with the loss of liquid. It was because he had been heading back towards Slubber.

He passed through the airlock and made his way to the palace. He entered the chamber where Slubber was asleep.

"Wake up, monster!" he cried.

Slubber opened bleary eyes. "What the hell?"

Frapper lifted the goblet high. "This is yours! It went on a journey with me and we had a very interesting time."

Slubber sat up. "Are you taking the—"

Frapper answered with a shout. "Yes! I took it. I took it and I've been bringing it back ever since. Now it is here!"

He emptied the goblet over Slubber's head.

One yellow drop hung suspended on the rim for what seemed an age. Then it fell, landing on the slob's brow and splashing there with a faint tinkle like a tiny chime officially announcing the end of the quest.

Frapper turned on his heel and strode out of the palace to face the citizens and explain to them that their planet wasn't flat after all.

FORBIDDEN FUTURES

RAY GUN FUN
FORBIDDENFUTURES.COM

THE MERROW AND HER SOLDIER
Cody Goodfellow

THE INTERSYSTEM GUNSHIP DAVID HUME DREW A BEAD ON LG-HYX233 AND SQUIRTED A STREAM OF SMART BULLETS AT THE TUMBLING ASTEROID. AT THE TERMINAL PHASE OF THE DROP, EACH BULLET WAS ONLY AS SMART AS ITS HUMAN PILOT, AND AT THIS LATE STAGE IN THE WAR, SMART PILOTS WERE HARD TO COME BY.

One in eight bullets collided almost immediately after deployment, and several more burst when they hit the halo of luminescent wreckage the others left behind. The surviving bullets blossomed with missile salvos when they hit the asteroid's eggshell atmosphere, layer upon layer of warheads erupting from within the insulation burning off their hulls. Under normal landfall protocols, the missiles—smarter by far than the average soldier—would lay down a tracking vector for the bullets to follow, but the enemy's inherent entropy played havoc with automated guidance systems. Besides, in the crystalline clarity of space, the luminous green witch-glow of the enemy's congregation circles paved the way for both dumb motion sensors and visual locks.

At the point of his squad's scattershot wedge formation, Corporal Ely Nunn struggled to stay in control and sort the conflicting voices in his head and his ears. His wetwiredear-bones throbbed with squad chatter, telemetry and armory stats from the bullethead, the barked commands and blasphemies of Sergeant Puckett, the jingle and clatter of fetishes and charms in his helmet. Cutting through it all, the siren song of the Merrow, keening through the cramped blackness of his cockpit, so that he could not, did not want to, hear anything else.

"God's balls, Quaker, wake the hell up! That's a collision alarm you're hearing! Heel off, boy! Toshi! Hey, Toilet-Boy, you're declination's too steep, your goddamn shell's melting! Flaco, mind the chaplain, he's going into an ecstasy again. Nunn? Corporal Nunn, why haven't you gone weapons hot yet?"

Nunn jolted back to awareness as the Sergeant's voice redoubled, keyed into the Corporal's personal channel, invoking pain protocols like a hive's worth of beestings in each ear. "NUNN, ARE YOU EXPERIENCING MALFUNCTION?"

Nunn swallowed hard to open the hailer in his larynx. "Momentary irresponse from armory menu, sir."

"Turn off the goddamned bullethead and be a soldier, son! You can't trust 'ware around the Sidhe, Corporal! Assume everything's dusted, Corporal Nunn, everything!"

"Sir, yes sir!"

"Good! Arm up and take point at landfall! Be a goddamn soldier, son!"

And he went out, leaving Nunn plummeting into the asteroid, drowning in song.

Pvt. Quaker laid down a scalar wave field that shivered the battlefield to dancing bits of obsidian dust. The ground tossed like a blanket on a laundry line, faultlines cresting and crashing into each other, sending debris rocketing out of atmosphere. Only the enemy stood fast, seeming to hover inches above the boiling rock, their massed voice a throbbing din that overloaded the bullets' sonic damping circuits: "Who disturbs our revelry? What offerings have you brought to the feast of the Good People?"

The bullets hit the ground more or less in formation just as the tremors subsided, anchored themselves in their craters in a hedgehog pattern and commenced lobbing everything they had over the rims.

Nunn leapt free of the crater, Phalanx Darts spitting out of his armor in all directions, and led the charge. The enemy swarmed the neutral zone, choosing to dance brazenly atop the broken cover supplied by Quaker instead of hide behind it. Autocannons unfolded from Nunn's shoulders and fired 24-inch iron stakes at the Sidhe, impaling a few, deflating them on the slightest contact. The Merrow's painsong jumbled his training, caused him to override the bullethead's target-readings and queer its aim. It was standard practice to second-guess the computer in this type of battle. Nunn told himself the bullethead might go rogue and select his comrades if it got fairy-dusted, so it could be worse. He was laying down suppressing fire; he was just a bad shot.

Naked, knobby gnomes scrambled out of the ground and danced round Pvt. Hideo, too close to him for Pvt. Jesus or T.S. Wombat to open fire, and sprayed him with a blizzard of the Dust. As his comrades deserted him, a bower of gorgeous Spring blossoms sprouted from every seam in Hideo's bullet: giant, luxuriant hothouse tulips, daffodils, crocuses and lilies of the valley, each with Hideo's weeping face at the center, pleading for mercy-killing.

Jabberjack ate his way out of the ground, up the leg of Pvt. Toshi and out the top of his helmet. Toshi's hailer-implant broadcasted his invectives, his screams, and the gurgling of Jabberjack's bottomless gullet.

Aiken Drum cut capers round the company, a jaunty elf dressed in finery made of delectable foodstuffs. His hand went to one pocket of his greatcoat made of lettuce leaves and sausages and took out a flute made from an eel. Quaker let fly a drum of teratogyn-B before he could sound a note. The livid red cloud enveloped Aiken Drum, but he capered out untouched, his edible suit sloughing off in wormy tatters. Quaker, Perspex and Jumblatt saw his nakedness and began to bark like mad dogs.

Pvt. Jesus lumbered out of formation, swatting at a cloud of sprites that taunted him with maddening jibes only he could hear. Jesus triggered his own Phalanx-Darts, one of which skewered Pvt. Perspex, while the rest simply turned on their source.

Salamanders, sporting in molten lava like salmon in a whitewater rapid, outflanked them, then dove out of sight. As the rest of the company fell back, Pvt. Flaco, engaged in tearing the legs off a sylph, lost his footing and sat down hard in a bubbling cauldron and sank out of sight, leaving only a puff of smoke. His cries went on regardless, distracting Nunn and the others with unwelcome thoughts of what the salamanders were doing to Flaco, that he was still screaming.

Nunn's piton-anchors deployed, rooting him to the smoking ground. The bullethead was off, its stand-&-fight scenarios disabled. The rock beneath him crumbled and dissolved. Almost relieved, Nunn toppled into blackness.

He hit the glassy smooth floor of a lava tube and bobsledded down the chute for several hundred yards before pulling himself together enough to redeploy pitons.

Nunn shut off his comm line and screamed, "What are you trying to do? Both sides'll want to kill us."

"I have offended you?"

"No... no, you haven't offended me. You just endangered both our lives. I'm supposed to be a soldier. You have to understand that."

"'Tis you, does not ken. I have no need of your protection; I remain only so long as it pleases me."

"You... can't go back—"

"You know well what I mean. Do not marry me to the death of my own kin. I need air." She unshipped the seals on Nunn's helmet. The transparent canopy retracted into the humpbacked dorsal plane of the bullet. Nunn gasped, not wanting to blow her out of his cockpit, not wanting to affright her away with the harsh words he held back.

The air was the same spicy atmosphere the Daoine Sidhe brought with them everywhere, the scent, some blasphemers said, of Old Earth. She stood on the lip of the cockpit, gazing down the endless lava tube, basking in his abasement. She began to sing again, and the sound of her voice carried him away just as his prox alarms began to blare.

"What the hell are you doing away from the fire zone, Corporal Nunn? Why have you depressurized your bullet, Nunn? What are you doing with... Holy fancy Moses—"

Sergeant Puckett came abreast of Nunn and unsealed his own cockpit, made ready to climb out of the suit and kick Nunn's ass when he saw her there. "Fraternizing with the enemy. I guess I still got a lot to learn about the weakness of spirit in degenerate pusbucket draftees. I want to thank you for teaching me a lesson, son. Pretty soon, we're getting vat-grown shocktroops anyway, so I don't suppose your kind'll be holding us back too much longer."

"No, Sarge, you don't understand! She's a captive. I'm grooming her as an informant."

"Your family don't never have to know nothing about this disgrace, Nunn," Puckett freed his arm from one hydraulic data-glove and produced a carbine pistol from his harness, a contraband insurance policy against ever being taken alive by the enemy. He pointed it at Nunn. Merrow shrilled a despairing cry, like a bird in the claws of a cat.

Something barreled down the black lava tube and alighted atop the Sergeant's carapace, knurled vulture's legs straddling the open cockpit like a cracked tortoise's shell. Puckett got two shots off into the featureless crotch of the interloper before it stooped over him and, unhinging its enormous jaw, bit his head neatly off at the base of his burly neck. Then its head got birdier, its wide jaws becoming a beak to burrow into his chest cavity. Nunn watched, paralyzed as much by Merrow's song as by his mingled horror and relief. The sergeant knew; the sergeant would kill him; the sergeant was dead.

The devourer emerged from the hollowed bullet smacking its tendriled lips, produced a faded burgundy stocking cap from a pocket, and dipped it in the pool of blood that was all that remained of Sgt. Amos Puckett. Chuckling wetly, the fairy barked a greeting to the Merrow, tugged the blood-dyed cap down onto its peaked head and fled gobbling down the tunnel.

War with the Daoine Sidhe began sixty years ago, and still no one knew quite what they were fighting, never mind why. Scant hours after the Royal Navy's W.B. Yeats became the first manned vessel to reach extrasolar space, she was boarded by the Good People, who summarily massacred her crew. Ship's logs could only describe the invaders in disjointed limerick-rhymes, but the physical evidence of the slaughter gave weight to their wildest couplets. But of the killers themselves, there was no sign.

Shortly afterward, the Sony automated factory-ship Zaibatsu touched down on the planet then known as Threshold and proceeded with its program of synthesizing durable consumer goods and a breathable atmosphere for colonists yet to arrive. Zaibatsu lost contact with Earth within days. When colonists set down, they also vanished, but not before reporting in that Fairies(!) had sabotaged Zaibatsu's programming, and to stay away at all costs. Threshold was nuked from orbit by the non-corporate Japanese torch-ship Aum, but glowing ghosts of the Good People, legends said, still haunted the ruin.

The military contingents of Earth's six space-faring powers took notice. The intergalactic diaspora had until then been seen by those capable of un-

dertaking it only as a path to new markets and penal colonies and disposable arenas in which to fight corporate wars. A common enemy threatening Earth's hegemony offered a hitherto unlooked for challenge, and one to which humans arose with renewed and savage vigor. Under the auspices of the Global Unification Pact, the Terran Colonial Navy set out with an armada of 176 torch-ships, carriers and unmanned Earth-Scorcher factory-ships to hunt the Good People. They found them everywhere, and nowhere at all. The more they encountered the enemy—and lost staggering casualties to them—the less they understood them.

There was no shortage of theories, of course. That the first ship to contact them was nominally British and named for a poet who authored a treatise on Irish folklore was held up by many as a sign that the Daoine Sidhe were nothing more than collective hysteria, brought on by overactive Celtic imaginations and the sanity-cracking stresses of interstellar travel. Zaibatsu's mainframe, however, was not programmed with Irish superstitions, and so the mythic nightmare it wrought on Threshold could only have been directed by a hostile agent,

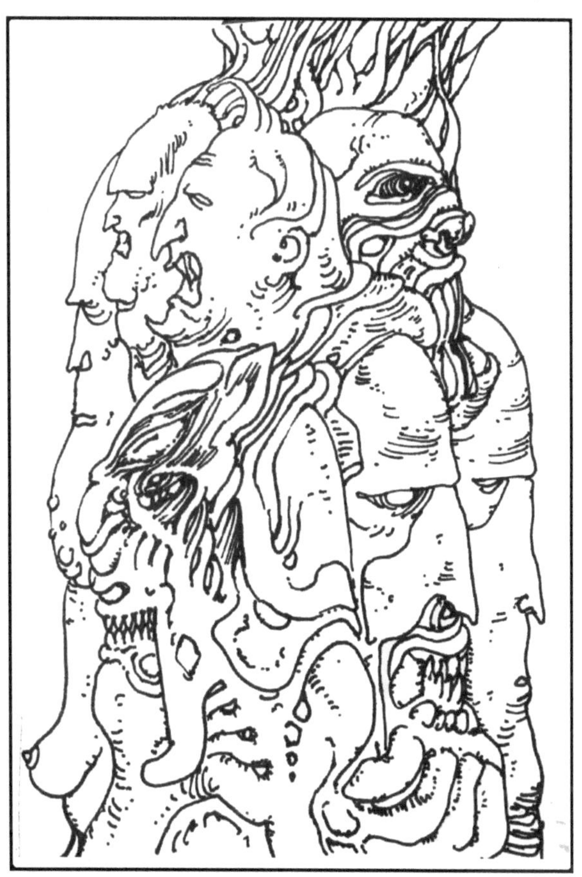

albeit one that wore the garb of Earth folklore. Stubborn adherents to the hysteria theory posited a species of psychoactive mimics whose first contact with a sentient race had warped their morphology into an approximation of the Good People. They speculated that, had an Islamic ship made the first contact, the Enemy would have been Djinns, talking pigs and Christians.

Others of a more sentimental bent believed that the Daoine Sidhe were the true Good People, who had fled the Earth before an increasingly rational and bloody-minded human race could vivisect them or smother them with skepticism. Perhaps they were the supernatural retribution for what men had done to the Earth itself. They were the fallen angels, the Nephilim, the forgotten gods of Earth, and man could no sooner fight a war against them than seek to shoot down the sun with rocks. But fight them they did.

And gradually, they began to win.

The Sidhe seemed simply to be wherever they wanted to be, without troubling with moving through space. Wherever a torch-ship put down on a backwater world, they were waiting, and sometimes simply walked onboard out of the depths of space. They were many-formed, seeming to boast

as many subspecies as humans had individuals, while some distinctive individual Faeries, such as Red Cap, Jabberjack, and Aiken Drum, seemed to appear on several worlds at once, and to die more times than could be recorded. They worked unimaginably strange weirds that made death irrelevant to them and merciful to men, and defended themselves in ways that made conventional weaponry worse than useless. The Good People seemed to have no homeworld (unless, as the Faerie-huggers had it, they came from Earth); no spacecraft, no technology and only one centralized monarchic court that had been briefly glimpsed by spy satellites on a hundred worlds, but never encountered in the flesh.

Of late, however, the tide had turned. As often as the Sidhe attacked, they seemed not to notice the humans at all, and allowed themselves to be slaughtered. The Colonial Navy didn't complain or second-guess the phenomenon, because they'd never beaten the Sidhe in a straight fight. It was only because the Sidhe seemed to have lost interest in the fight that the Navy could reasonably claim to be winning the war. The Good People only appeared in unsettled places, and pavement, particle physics, and pretzel stands seemed to be an implacable defense against them. Colonization was aggressively stepped up, with the Colonial Navy increasingly becoming a side-endeavor, genetically engineered soldiers and unwanted backwater riff-raff tooling around the fringes of the Empire looking to stamp out the last vestiges of the Daoine Sidhe, whom some had taken to calling the Dodos.

None of this mattered to Ely Nunn, who was in love.

Corporal Nunn clambered up out of the lava tube just as the retreat siren sounded. Numb, he let the bullet find its own way back to the rendezvous point and dock with the lander. Moving in under the apron of the lander's suppressing fire, Nunn saw thousands of Sidhe wading in after him, being pounded to mulch even as they cut a Maypole Dance around the lander. In a few minutes the dance would open a Door beneath the ship, and it would fall in, or something unspeakable would crawl out of it and smash them to bits. They would not be there when it opened; only five other soldiers had survived. Within seconds, they were all loaded and the lander took off, lobbing dirty nukes in its wake. The Door had opened, and none of the bombs detonated, but simply dropped into the swirl of otherworldly color they were ordered never to look into. He read the names of the other survivors: Walden, Huygens, Mbunta, Jumblatt and Quaker. Three were grievously injured and pumped up on meds. The latter two were sedated by their own bullets in the field, and would remain so forever, lest they spread their madness. The others talked among themselves. Nunn wanted to log on, see if they were talking about him, dreaded that they would be, that they knew.

"Merrow?"

"I am yours."

"Sing me a song."

In his cubicle, the Merrow came out of her hiding place. She was tiny, even by the standards of her kind, as tall as Nunn's hand. Her lithe form was covered from head to toe in glistering, opalescent scales. Their colors betrayed her mood: a livid amaranthine spoke of her anguish and fierce anger at the dreadful losses inflicted on her kin. But veins of longed-for aquamarine penetrated the stormy violet, pleading with him to be kind. His own anger leached away as hers diffused into shades of passivity.

"Do not be cross with me, my lord. I only thought to save you."

"We were seen together. The Sarge might've been transmitting. As soon as the battle tapes are reviewed, the whole fleet'll know." Would they come for him, or simply gas him in his sleep? He had no idea how traitors would be handled, because he'd never heard of anyone betraying his own kind for the Daoine Sidhe. If nothing else, he was a pioneer.

"None of your devices ring true in the presence of the Sidhe," she said. "They'll see nothing, or they'll see lies, and there's an end on it."

"There's no end to it. I can't keep you a secret forever."

"You've no ken what forever is. Forever eats you."

He looked at his big, coarse hands, and wished they were small enough to caress her, or large enough to crush himself. "You must hate me."

"I am made to be with you." Her scales shaded mauve with naked sadness.

"You're not my slave," he said, voice breaking. "You could leave. You choose to stay—"

"And why do you have me to stay? I am the foe of your kind."

"I—I love you. You know love, don't you? You can feel love?"

"I am love. I know of nothing else. I have the seas of Earth in my tears, but no memories. I doubt but that I never abode there. The ones among you who say that we are your dreams made flesh by your fears and hates, I fear that this is so. That is why we fought you, and now have all but quit, and that is why I stay. Your kind dreams, and then you kill them. It hurts to be someone's dream."

He reached out his hand to stroke her luminous scales. She shrank away, turning scarlet under his callused hand as if he burned her with his touch. "I could never have dreamt someone like you, but we can't stay together like this. It's—it's not natural."

She laughed, her voice too bright with gall to express itself in color. "We were once the Tuatha-De-Danaan, and worshiped as gods; even then, we took lovers among mortals, and made heroes and monsters. When you forgot us, we shrank,

but still we were the Good People. We would not be forgotten again." Her tone and scales softened. "Aye, humans and Sidhe have paired. The Good People of Earth sometimes would steal human babes, and replace them with their own, or with a stick or a toad in the manger—" She trailed off, then looked at him.

"I must tell you something that will wound you, Ely Nunn," she murmured, her tongue charging his name with power. She had never bound him by his name before, and she had known it from their first meeting, on his first engagement with the enemy, when he had thought he captured her.

"The Good People will come for me tonight."

Was she joking? He couldn't breathe. "They'll never get you. They could walk into this cubicle, but they'd never walk out."

"They will come and take me away. They would not see me the concubine of a slayer of my own kin."

"And would you go with them?"

"I would go only by your leave, if such were so, but what skills it for my will to be heard, that weighs but naught? I would lief die, than see them kill thee, for I am made to abide with you. But there is another way."

Too eagerly, he asked, "What is it?"

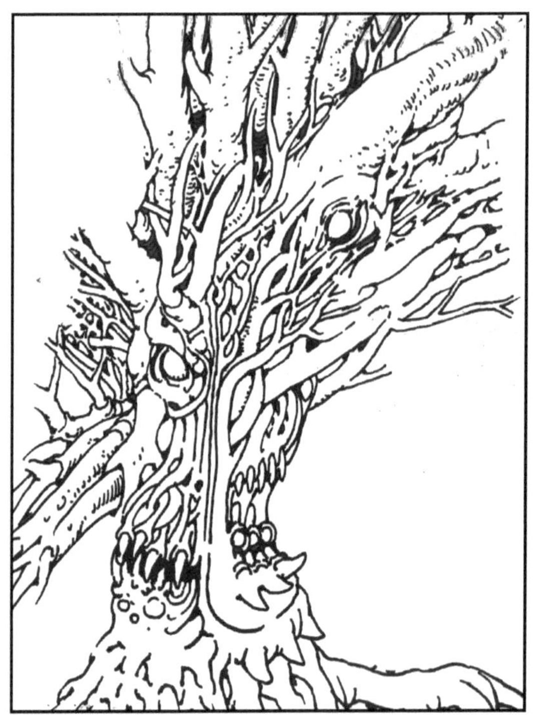

"They would set a task upon you."

"What task?"

"Let them tell it."

A shadow deepened and spread out of one corner of his cubicle, became blacker, became a door. A procession of Daoine Sidhe stepped out of the black, seemed to flow back into it, to the back of infinity. He'd heard tales of the Gentry, a tribunal of elder representatives of the chief subspecies of the Sidhe. They appeared before high naval officers in their quarters at the hearts of the most densely protected gunships, even on the flagship. They came to them in dreams and judged them for crimes against the Good People. A few had been found innocent, and were summarily executed by the Navy. The rest were found in their beds, slain by a fright that left their hair white and their burst hearts still leaping about on the floor. Spreading such tales was itself a kind of treason, but word still leaked out. Fear clutched Corporal Nunn as they fixed their withering gazes upon him.

One of the Gentry raised its voice in a gurgling sing-song that spoke of briny depths and earthen labyrinths, forgotten frontiers on an abandoned homeworld. His Merrow's scales went silver with a longing so pure she seemed about to vanish. Thinking they were taking her from him, Nunn shouted, "Leave her be! She is my thrall! You have no power over her any more!"

A gnome rolled his bullseye-lamp orbs and plucked his mossy beard, laughing. "Moosha! He stands upon his head, and the sun shines out his arse!"

A ghastly, icthyoid creature hauled itself up out of the horde, its goggling, piggish eyes stretching out of its face to regard Nunn in stereo profile, its clump of suckered snouts and gills flaring livid purple with blood and jealous rage. Another Merrow. Nunn had read in his Yeats manual that the males were not so beautiful as the female. "You own her so long as you know her name... and has she told it to you?"

He started to nod, but their laughter cut his strings.

"You are free so long as you love her not, manchild. And if you love her... you are hers!" They all took up his chuckling.

"What do I have to do?"

The gnome plucked one of the toadstools blooming from a cranny of his gnarled skull and gnawed on it. "Only open a Door for us."

"But I don't know anything about magic!"

"Wise enough are we in those ways. But we can't open the Door to that nowhere you lot have made to keep your lore."

"You mean the noosphere, right? I don't know any more about that than I do about your magic." The fleet noosphere was a shared data-space, wherein communications were shared instantly across light years of interstellar space. Noosphere techs were shamanic monks; none saw them, let alone learned their trade.

"Aye," the bull-Merrow rasped, reining in his disgust. "You must open the ear of your lore-space, that we may whisper into it a secret."

"We want you to know where the High Court of the Faerie Queene lies." A slender pixie, translucent flesh a display case for his liquid gold innards, dropped a single disk on the deck, identical to those issued to each trooper for accessing bullethead modules and storing training scenario data.

Nunn found himself reaching for it even before he thought it out. "Why do you want us to know where to find your queen? We're already kicking your asses. It'd all be over. Is that what you want?"

They all laughed heartily again, a raucous music that set the room spinning. "Winning?" snorted the bull-Merrow. "The longer you fight, the more you believe in us. The more you believe, the more our legions grow."

The pixie silenced him with a wave and a sprinkle of dust. "We grow weary of fighting our common cousins. We are joined, and spilled blood is the blood of us all."

A leprechaun lighted his pipe off the lambent blue flames of the Salamander beside him. "She will take terms for our surrender or offer up her throat, as is her wont," he grumbled around the stem, crowning himself with garlands of green-black smoke. "The war will end, the killing of men and Sidhe and worlds will cease. And the Merrow-daughter will be yours."

"I don't believe you. I know about dealing with the Good People."

"Aye, an' you're neck-deep in dealing!" the Gnome cackled. "You've claim to none of the nay-sayin' here!"

"Put him under spells and crosses to do the thing!" the bull-Merrow barked, and his colors seemed an attack meant to blind him.

"I will not, his Merrow-daughter murmured, by which all present knew what was meant. "Please, Ely," she whispered, and began to sing.

He went to the training center. He recognized none of the other troopers waiting to enter the danger rooms, and stepped into line for a terminal. He gripped the disk in his hand, which tried to break it and cut the knot for him. Was this an act of betrayal, or heroism? Disaster, or the end of the war? Was it both?

He slotted his disk, expecting something unusual to happen. His stats came up, with a menu of scenarios and skill levels. The image fluctuated a bit for a moment, as if some enormous drain on the fleet memory was passing through, but then went steady. Sweating, Nunn selected a medium-level deep space skirmish. When his turn came, he entered the danger room and climbed into a pod. The familiar sinking feeling as the vapor-mask pressed over his face, and he slipped into a trance.

The scenarios were an empty ritual, useless as preparation for true combat against the Good People. No computer could extrapolate a realistic model of Sidhe strategy, no matter how insane its programmer, and replays of previous battles only taught trainees how to massacre an unresisting, oblivious foe, or to accept inevitable slaughter by creatures out of nightmare. Still, even empty rituals had to be observed. Hollow observances, mundane things, it was whispered, kept the Sidhe away.

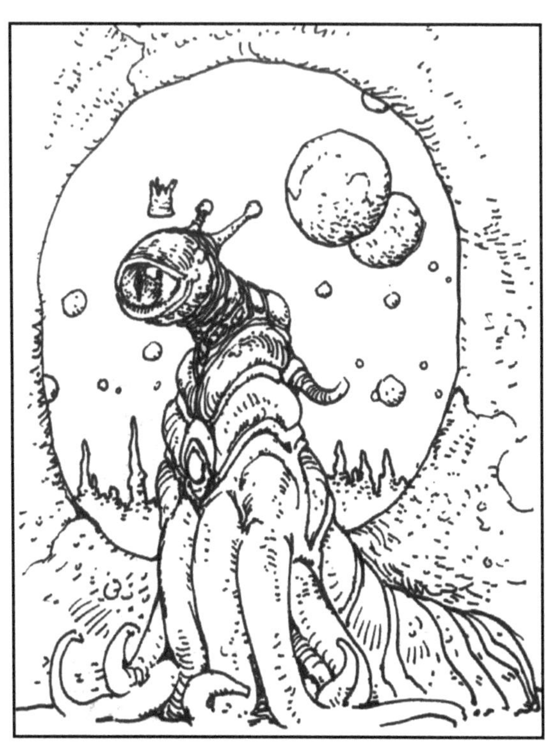

Halfway through the scenario, the claxons sounded general quarters. Arm smarting from the stimulant injection that brought him out of the scenario, he scrambled back to his cubicle. In the midst of the sirens and bells, an intercom voice purred into his ear implant, "Corporal Nunn, report to command center terminal immediately."

He was caught. Should he go meekly to his execution, or should he die with his Merrow, at least to see one last time the creature that had bewitched him into betraying his own race?

He jacked into a command terminal off the main corridor, was instantly sucked into the submenu of fleet command, passed up the chain of command so fast he was given a mental nosebleed. He arrived at a virtual office, a colossal affair of somber black marble, a mausoleum haunted by thousands of flittering ghosts–other meetings taking place in the same space.

An officer stood atop a platform in the center, resplendent in a single spotlight of pure Earthly sunlight, which picked out the treasure-trove of medals and insignia on his chest. Troopers never saw commanding officers in the flesh. For the protection and security of all, they only appeared in the noosphere, safe from Sidhe assassination. Some said the last officers had been wiped out by the Gentry long ago, and the war was now being run by their ghosts, data imprints stored in the noosphere.

"Corporal Ely Nunn. You know why you are here."

"Um–yes, sir. I mean, I'm not sure–"

"Your squad was wiped out in the engagement on Lg-HyX233. You are the only man who returned with body and mind intact. Do you know why that was the case?"

"No, sir. I tried, I really did."

"We know you did. You have superior survival skills, Corporal. Simulation scenarios project that had you been in command of the squad, casualties would have been reduced by 65 percent. We'd like to rectify the situation immediately. You are now Sergeant Major Nunn, and will immediately take command of a full platoon of shocktroops."

"Sir?"

"A major offensive is in the offing, Sergeant. The entire fleet is regrouping for what may prove to be the climactic engagement of the war." He hung his head at the bittersweet prospect. "The ultimate offensive. The objective is the Court of the Faerie Queene. One final push, and human hegemony will be unquestioned throughout the universe."

"Sir, I never thought it would go this far. I want to turn myself in–"

"That's the spirit. We want you to lead the charge. We hit the throneworld in thirty-six hours. You'll just have enough time to undergo non-comm imprinting and review your new platoon. Congratulations, Sergeant Major."

Nunn wandered back to his cubicle to find his belongings–dress uniform, fatigues, mess kit and his collection of wards and charms–packed up in his rucksack. His Merrow knelt on the bag, her scales shimmering with nameless colors, a prism of emotions beyond the ken of mortals. She seemed to look through him, a ghost filled up with love and made to beguile mortals, but incapable of returning it. For good or ill, with magic or with the weakness of his own mind, she had used him. He could understand none of the rest of it. But this one thing he could get his head around, and for the sake of his own sanity, he had to act on it.

"You tricked me," he growled, forcing his voice low for as long as he could. "You're all lies. You're made of them, it's all you know how to do."

All over, she turned the color of fresh bruises. "It's for the good of your people as well as my own. And we can be together." Words failed her, and she fell into a plaintive, keening song. She was trying to charm him again; she was calling back the Gentry, who had no more use for him. A Faerie couldn't be trusted. They had the Devil's own cunning, and no souls of their own to lose by using it. Big, slow, stupid and mortal though he was, he believed that he had a soul, and a need to cleanse it.

"You don't have to sing, anymore, Merrow. You only have to say my name." He took her in his hands and held her up to the light. "You can stop me, Merrow, you can order me to die... Just say... my... name..." He closed his eyes, clenched his jaw to damp down his earphones. As he began to squeeze her, he could hear only the roaring of his blood inside him.

She gasped, but made no other sound. Tears streamed down her tiny doll's cheeks, melting her. She dissolved in briny tears, a fistful of seawater from a dead world.

Nunn wiped his hands on the mat, whispered a prayer for the first time in his life, and, shouldering his bag, left the cubicle.

Nunn spent twelve hours in deep sleep for his non-commissioned officer imprinting. He awoke a Sergeant Major, ready to lead men into battle. He entered the flight deck programmed to feel confident of snatching decisive victory out of the teeth of the worst possible scenario. Even one that was, very likely, a trap into which he himself had led the entire Terran fleet. A holographic officer standing at attention on his holographic platform saluted him. Behind him stood rank upon rank of identical soldiers, whose synchronized salute made Nunn think he was in a hall of mirrors.

Sgt. Maj. Nunn returned the salute, approached his men with a veteran officer's eye superimposed on his own. The men were perfection: chiseled, bird-boned forms, gracefully elongated for extended tours in deep space. Their honey-golden eyes fluttered behind nictitating membranes, which darkened in bright light. They looked less human than most Faeries did.

"These aren't the dregs you're used to fighting with, Sergeant. These are genetically engineered soldiers, of the highest germline stock yet manufactured. They'll imprint on your commands like the word of God, and they'll serve you well. You'll be the first of seventy-seven squadrons of air-to-ground troopers, with full orbital artillery support. Intel so far is, um, sketchy, but projections put a Host of at least fifty thousand enemy combatants on the ground, with the Queene. And they're torpid. All signs show they won't even put up a fight."

Falling into a corkscrew orbit round the Sidhe throneworld, Nunn chatted up his men, who were strangely silent. "60! Get up in front–good job. 32! Stop that–okay." They anticipated his commands, flowing into the mission like one body, with him a redundant accessory yapping at their exhaust.

Then, at the outer skin of the atmosphere, his formation flew apart, splaying off in all directions, dodging each other and coming back at him at twice their falling speed, firing their autocannons for propulsion. Nunn whirled out of their path as they turned back on the fleet. All across the horizon, the other elite squads did the same.

The Good People on Earth would sometimes steal human babes, and replace 'em with their own

Nunn switched to the officer's comm channels and tried to make himself heard, but his voice was lost among the chorus of Faerie-song blaring from every commander's bullet except his own.

SAFEWORD

K.H. KOEHLER

"The safeword is 'Barbarella.'"

He stumbles over the word as I shove the ball-gag deep into his mouth. I expect him to react and point out the obvious issue with our arrangement: If he can't talk, he can't give me his safeword. But M'tha'lu isn't the sharpest warlord in the drawer.

He does have a soft spot for some pretty specific kink, though.

After the green bastard is secured to the bondage table, I flip it over. A large window has been cut out of the table, exposing his back and buttocks. This works because I can do my work without looking at his face--which is a blessing, trust me.

Dr. Brian Mafune, my esteemed creator, designed me with an almost entirely organic quicksilver body, so it doesn't take long to sploosh to the top of the table and realign my particles accordingly. M'tha'lu likes Jane Fonda in four-inch dominatrix heels, so I create a proxy just in case he has eyes in his ass that I haven't spotted.

My memories of the actress are gleaned from stolen satellite broadcasts and lone VHS copies salvaged from the trash collectors who hit Earth after the Long War. Long yellow hair and lioness eyes. Silver skin and big, useless boobs and guns.

M'tha'lu moans in delight as I walk back and forth in the heels, hitting what I hope are the erogenous zones on his spongy green misshapen body. I'm doing a pretty solid job; I can barely hear the Electronica pulsing from the club beyond the door for the sounds he's making.

They remind me of a cat coughing up a hairball.

I stomp back and forth like a fashion droid on a squishy catwalk. When the knock falls on the door, I pause. "Occupied," I say through my translator so it comes out in the spittle-y warlord's language in case it's one of his flunkies.

"We come inside you now," the mechanical reply echoes from the other side of the door.

A droid. Its translator is busted or he's using words that the device has to approximate in Earth-speak.

"How 'bout you fuck off, friend?"

"You come open."

"Learn to speaken ze English."

Fuck. My big mouth. When Dr. Mafune designed me, he reversed the programming he used to create my predecessor, Number Thirteen. He thought Thirteen was too soft. He wasn't wrong. But the snark doesn't help. Particularly in these delicate situations.

A tingle in my spine gives me advance warning, but it isn't enough for when the droid opens fire on the door, shredding the metal iris and the rounded, egg-like walls of the private room. Fiery projectiles rip past and through me.

They punch ragged, burning holes in my body stuff. The sound is deafening and I feel as if I have bees in my brain. The impacts drive my remnants to the floor beside the bondage table.

My vision swims with darkness until my nanos kick in and I form a pair of working eyes. I'm under the table, looking up at M'tha'lu's stark, terrified face. He's bitten right through the ball-gag, which hangs in tatters. "B-Barbarella..." he babbles through a panic-rictured mouth."Barbarella...Barbarella!"

Not a droid, my rebooted brain blinks alive. "Assassin."

I know I'm right. M'tha'lu is wanted throughout the quadrant for various war crimes. Why not get 'im when he's vulnerable? And if the sex worker gets it, who gives a shit, right?

Collateral damage pisses me off. I surge like a waterfall over the bondage table and extend my arm toward the assassin. My nanos swarm and reconfigure my arm into the biggest-ass hand cannon I can possibly imagine.

The assassin lowers his gun. I see now that he's flesh and blood. A ballistic plastic war suit and helmet have given him the courage he needs to blow away a warlord and his whore. I know that suit can sustain a small nuclear strike.

"Feel lucky, punk?" Another line I picked up from a salvaged Earth movie.

His mouth makes a large "O" behind his plastic face shield. But I obliterate it—and the rest of him—with the first, searing blast of the sonic boom gun in my hand.

The dust settles both literally and figuratively, and I see that half of the club is gone.

Shit. Collateral. Well, do as I say, kittens, not as I do.

M'tha'lu is lying amidst the splintered refuse of the table.

"Th-th-thank you, Mistress." He crawls to me and grasps my hand so he can rest his squishy head against it.

I turn that hand into a manacle and chain that quickly ensnares the warlord's neck, jerking his head up. I see the pleasure on his face, but I know something that will get him even more hot and bothered.

I produce my marshal's badge from my self-stuff. "M'tha'lu, you are under arrest for war crimes against the Alliance..."

I Only Saw You

David James Keaton

THE FIRST TIME I SEE YOU, I'M ONLY A BOY, but I know what I saw. Ironically, it's only later, when all doubt is erased, that I suddenly become unconvinced. Or maybe it's the other way around.

As a kid, I got car-sick so frequently I'd pretend I was a time traveler used to riding horses instead, or riding the alien equivalent of a horse, and I'm on the verge of puking when we see the rest stop and idling trucks, and my dad urges us to get some sleep, too. It's the first time I remember sleeping without a clock, and I worry this will mess me up forever. But it's also close enough to time travel to comfort me into a surprisingly restful slumber.

The next morning, I'm weirdly excited when we're stuck in a construction bottleneck with the same semis we'd nested with. Boxed in like a turtle, we're trapped with trucks crawling slow as tanks, blocking traffic before the highway turns into a single lane. Restless, Dad plays with the vents, and I imagine him activating the afterburners. A sign says the exit's two miles ahead, and he's relieved to finally ease over toward the right. But as soon as we head for that shoulder, the big red truck in front of us belches smoke and swerves to block our path, quicker than I'd have thought possible.

My dad hisses like a snake under a boot heel and tries the left, but the trailer whiplashes to block us again. This goes on for a while, until Dad feints left, then right, then zips by the semi, shaking a victory fist. We fly through the glorious empty lane, since congestion had cleared about three football fields worth of blacktop, and I lean out my window to yell back to everyone, "Don't worry! We'll send help from the future!"

I'm still hanging out the window like a dog when I see the cop behind us.

So Dad's explaining the history of 18-wheelers' disregard for the law while the cop at his window keeps repeating, "I only saw you, sir. I only saw you, sir…"

She ends up citing him for reckless operation. Meanwhile, the trucks have time to catch up, and that big red truck gives us a big red honk as it rumbles by, air brakes practically snickering. The cop sees this and takes off, her cherries flashing back on as she pulls over our nemesis, tables turned again. And when the traffic jam inches us up to them, the driver's outside with her, huge trailer doors open. The driver is a big man in a white jumpsuit, and I'm now thinking astronaut thoughts instead of time traveler thoughts and holding my breath to see if Dad will honk. Instead, we watch those big doors slam shut.

I'm convinced he saw what I saw in the back of that truck, because his hand hovers over the horn for a quarter mile before it slowly returns to the steering wheel. The exit never seems to come.

For years, we'd sometimes guess what was in people's trunks, and this seemed like the ultimate culmination of that game, the final boss. But later when I ask, he denies everything. So I convince myself it was fantasy, or a fake, maybe a huge parade statue, or a monster for a Mardi Gras. Hollow, at the very least, because I'd never seen a spaceman the size of a school bus. And certainly never one with a grin like yours...

I spin around to look for the red truck, my carsick stomach back in knots. Dad catches my eye in the rearview mirror and says nothing. That night, on the side of the road again, I can't sleep and watch them rumble by, fingers and nose over the seat like Kilroy, looking at those trailers in a whole new light, and I think of the dangers of night skies and roads out of time.

THE LAST TIME I SEE YOU, I'm working a plumbing stint in the ass end of east Toledo. Every time my boss gets Long John Silver's, I steal time off his clock talking to the chubby, sad-faced neighborhood kid, giving him my Big Gulp cup to collect all the bones the neighborhood dogs stashed after the house was condemned, promising to make a dinosaur for him when he's done.

Grateful for the attention, the kid brings me a gift, placing the plastic bubble from a gumball machine so carefully in my hand that I think it contains something alive.

"When I was young, we got stuff to eat out of those eggs," I say. "And we were thankful!" But sometimes we got spacemen.

Inside is a little plastic gang member with a red bandanna—"Homies," I think they call them—and I forget about it until he brings another the next day, presenting it with all the ceremony of a Congressional Medal of Honor. It's another little plastic gangbanger, but in a tiny plastic wheelchair. The kid calls him, "The King," and I ask if his little homunculus took a bullet to the spine. Confused, the kid says, "Naw, that's his throne."

"Thanks for the King, kid," I say, and keep digging. All week, he brings me more gangsters in bubbles; one selling oranges, one weightlifting, one spraying graffiti, one with a pimp chalice, one weird outer space alien gangster, even one with a little alligator on a leash.

The day my shovel finds you is the day the kid comes back for his King. He tells me he'd gave me the wrong toy by mistake and hands me a plastic bubble with a small skull inside the size of a lizard egg, a Homie's head with Day of the Dead facepaint.

"What's this, a Halfway Homie?" I joke, but he's deadly serious, and it's all heads in the bubbles after that. I line the heads along the basement wall so we have an audience while I dig my PVC trench, sometimes hitting a rib or a chicken bone, and those he lines up, too, our basement a bit like a ceremonial alter now. We take turns guessing what dinosaur it will eventually become.

When I'm on the last curve of my trench, my shovel hits the biggest bubble of them all, and the children's games are over.

At first I think it's glass from an old basement window, because I see the curve of concrete foundation about a half foot below it. Then I realize it's not concrete but bone beneath that glass. Thick bone. Your massive skull, of course, once white, now grey, leering up at me from under your bubble. Another two shovelfuls and I see your head's not in a state of decay after all. It's a skull never meant to be hidden, not beneath a layer of muscle or skin, or in a helmet, or even a truck. This is your face in life, not in death, and the smile you wear was not incidental.

When my boss comes down smoking a fish stick, he spits it out, steps past us, then screams for me to look look! behind me where I know you're pulling yourself free of your tomb with fingertips the size of mailboxes.

"We don't work for you anymore," I say, the kid at my side. I see the flash of my screwdriver in the kid's fist, and I grip my shovel with both hands.

Once we lay the old boss in the trench, we wait until night, no need for a clock anymore. We leave you in the dark because we know more of you are waiting. We move to the next house, to the next basement, another new boss.

Digging faster now, the boy presses another toy into my hand, but when I look, I only see you.

"While we were on spring break in Cancun, we met this dude who looks just like Jesus."

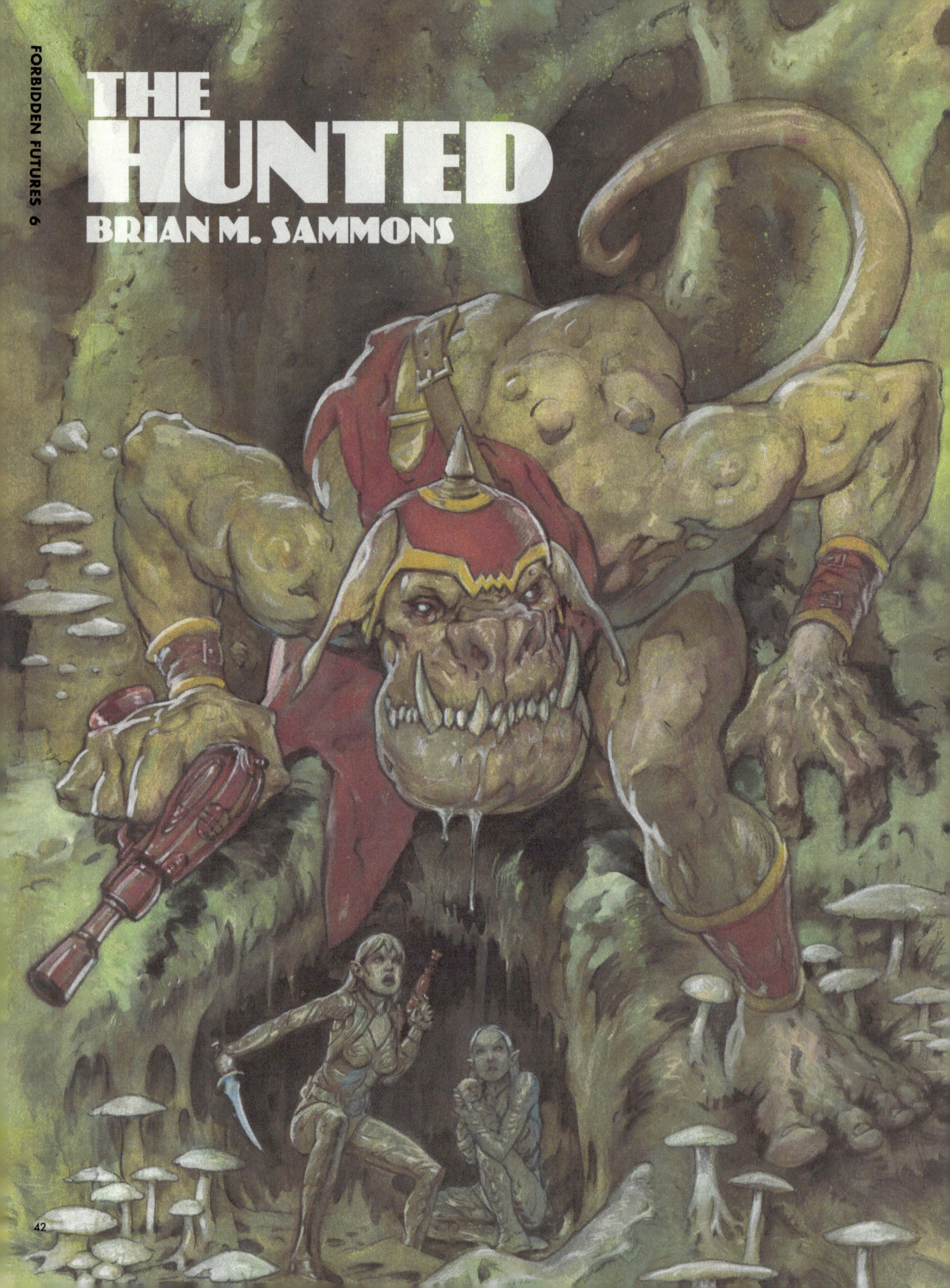

FORBIDDEN FUTURES 6
THE HUNTED
BRIAN M. SAMMONS
42

THE BEAM OF CRIMSON LIGHT STREAKED OVER NANDRA'S LEFT SHOULDER WITHOUT SO MUCH AS A WHISPER.

Unlike the old slug-throwers of generations past, there was no boom of thunder or puff of smoke to give away the position of the one that had just shot at her. No, masers, phasers, and in this case, lasers were nothing but focused energy, and specifically the laser was only light. Light makes no sound, so the weapons that utilized them were all the more effective for their silence.

"Damn, that was close," Zellman said, noticing the flash of red as well. He and Nandra were squatting behind fallen, fungus-covered tree trunks, hoping they had lost the quellian when they had seen it slip and fall down the rocky hillside. But no such luck. He had found them, again, with only his torn shirt looking the worse for wear. He even had his stupid pointy hat still on its canid-shaped head.

"Come on, we got to move," Nandra said, but Zellman placed a trembling hand on her knee, keeping her still.

"I don't think I can," the man said, nodding to his left ankle that he had twisted and torn in flight up the same stony hill that had toppled their pursuer. But whereas quellians had thick, leathery skin and bones with the equivalent density of carbon steel, humans only had soft flesh and bones that snapped with little effort.

"We can't stay here, he clearly saw us enough to take a shot."

Zellman gave it a moment of thought and then said, "Okay, give me a hand."

Nandra nodded and helped the man up. He was her subordinate, and quite frankly, she never did like him much. Too much frat boy he had yet to grow out of. But they were the last two left, and she might need his help to take down the twenty-two-foot-tall "perfect predator" that was after them.

"You think something that big, someone would have shot him by now," Nandra mused out loud to herself.

"Gatordogs are great in the reflexes department. Comes from living on a hellhole of a planet where everything wants to eat you." Zellman said, allowing himself to vent a little frustration by using a speciesist slur for quellians that had gone out of style three decades ago.

The two limped their way deeper into the musty-smelling grove. It had been her idea to hide there, hoping that the fungal spores would cover their scent and give them some advantage over the quellian, whose olfactory sense was known to be ten times better than Earth canines.

"Hey, look," Zellman whispered, pointing over his shoulder at something.

Nandra let the man down easy and turned to see the quellian. He was on all fours, keeping low in the tall grass, but she could see his head and shoulders peeking up as he sniffed the air for them.

I knew it, Nandra thought as she pulled her own laser pistol from her holster.

"What are you doing?" the man next to her asked.

"Taking the shot."

"What? He's too far. You'll miss."

"Shhhh," she hissed, lining up the weapon's sights on the lantern-jawed, snaggletoothed visage some eighty meters distant.

"Don't."

"Shut up, we may not get another chance..."

"All you're going to do is piss him off." Zellman pleaded, "Don't risk it."

Perfect predator, my ass, Nandra thought and gently squeezed the trigger.

And missed with her own crimson lance of light.

Almost instantly, the quellian's head ducked back down and she could tell by the way the chest-high grass parted that he was coming right for them. Fast.

"Oh shit," she said. "Come on." She reached to pull Zellman up to run, but he only made it halfway up before a laser struck him in the back. The man's teeth clamped together as pain wracked his body, his muscles tensed, and Nandra dropped him. She instinctively went to pick him up again when he said through clenched teeth: "Noooooo, ruuuuun."

Nandra let out a single sob, nodded, turned, and then ran like the Devil himself was chasing her.

No, worse, she thought bitterly, *that perfect predator son of a bitch.*

She threw her arms up to protect her face as she went smashing through the undergrowth and low-hanging branches draped in stinging thorn-moss. Two more bolts of red light missed her by inches on either side as she fled, and she could hear the hulking quellian gaining on her.

"Nandra, you're the lasssst," she heard him hiss out with a sloppy lisp all quellians were known for. That's what happened when you had a mouthful of fangs, some as long as three feet. "Lassssst one sssstanding."

"Up yours!" Nandra yelled out, knowing that she should save her raw, ragged breath for running, but she couldn't not say something to that smug asshole. Besides, she knew the end was coming soon. She could feel it. Just like she could hear her pursuer give a sibilant laugh. Yeah, he was having a great time, she thought.

Then came the pain: sharp, sudden, electric, and Nandra knew she had been shot. She collapsed to the ground, her legs cramping up and failing her. Her teeth clenched on a protest stuck in her throat that she couldn't spit out. As she lay there, convulsing, something large and squamous blocked out the sun. The quellian towered above her, now standing at his full height, a drool-dripping grin over his tusked maw.

"Got you," he said with the smile spreading.

"Well that's it, Grellwer wins… again," someone called out, followed by a chorus of halfhearted congratulations from all those that had previously been shot by the quellian.

"Thank you, thank you," Grellwer the quellian said to the humans coming out of the treeline as Nandra slowly got to her feet. The shock vest she wore having run through its thirty second immobilization cycle, she could once again stand.

"Man, these vests are bullshit. The pain induction is turned up too high," said Zellman, echoing Nandra's thoughts as he was being carried forward by two of his coworkers.

"That'sssss the incentive not to get sssssshot. Addssssss realisssssm." Grellwer said, still grinning, as he holstered his laser pistol.

"How would you know? You never get shot." Nandra said, then pointed her own laser gun at the giant and pulled the trigger. It didn't fire, not that she expected it to. Once the round was over,

or before that if someone was "killed," the lasers switched off automatically until the start of the next round.

"Hey, I can't help it if I am…" the big lizard started, and in unison a half dozen weary and angry voices joined in with, "the Perfect Predator."

There was a round of some not-so-good-natured laughing, followed by Grellwer hissing, "Well that'sssssss why I made management and the ressssssst of you didn't, I guesssss."

Grellwer paused after that, his mind racing. He wasn't as brutish as his race looked, and he sensed the animosity quickly rise in his human co-workers over his last remark, so he tried to lighten the mood. "And hey, Nandra, you almosssst got me when that rock turned under my foot on that hill and I fell back. Hell, I nearly broke my neck. I mean, look at me!" The quellian raised his arms to show off his ripped tunic.

"Too bad you didn't," Zellman said under his breath, but purposely not too under his breath.

Grellwer cleared his throat, "Well come on, we've got three more coursessssss to run and corporate wantsssss ussss to do them all before the sssssshuttle comessss to take ussss home."

A collective groan went through the assembled human employees of Smith, Tanaka, Miller, & Zas'kel'throol.

"Now sssssstop that," the quellian said. "Thisssss issss sssssuposssssed to bring ussssss clossssssser together asssss a team. And that will bring our numbersssss up, which you all know we need." He removed his ripped shirt, lest it impede his movements in the coming hunt. "Zellman, you can sssssit thissss round out. Get sssssome morpho sssspray on that leg. Assss for the ressssst of you, I'll give you a twenty minute head sssssstart this time, insssssstead of ten. Jussssst don't tell anyone, okay?" The towering reptile said, trying his best to sound magnanimous. But just like all those human words it spoke, it just didn't come out right, with all those fangs.

CREDITS

BRIAN M. SAMMONS is a fiction editor for Dark Regions Press and Chief Editor for Golden Goblin Press. His short fiction has appeared in such anthologies as Arkham Tales, Horrors Beyond, Monstrous, Mountains of Madness, Deepest, Darkest Eden and others. He has edited the books; Undead & Unbound, Eldritch Chrome, Edge of Sundown, Steampunk Cthulhu, World War Cthulhu, Flesh Like Smoke, Return of the Old Ones, Children of Gla'aki, and more. He is currently far too busy for any sane man. For more about this guy that neighbors describe as "such a nice, quiet man" you can follow him on Twitter @ BrianMSammons

DAVID JAMES KEATON'S fiction has appeared in over 100 publications, and his first collection, Fish Bites Cop! Stories to Bash Authorities (Comet Press), was named The Short Story Collection of the Year by This Is Horror. His second collection of short fiction, Stealing Propeller Hats from the Dead (PMMP) received a Starred Review from Publishers Weekly. He is also co-editor of the anthology Hard Sentences: Crime Fiction Inspired by Alcatraz (Broken River Books), and editor of Dirty Boulevard: Crime Fiction Inspired by the Songs of Lou Reed (Down & Out Books). He teaches composition and creative writing at Santa Clara University in California and can be found at davidjameskeaton.com

TONY MCMILLEN is the author of the heavy metal horror novel An Augmented Fourth and Nefarious Twit, a novel about murder and children's literature. He's also the artist and writer behind the rainbow oil slick hued dark fantasy comic book series Lumen and currently working on a comic about three decades of life in the practical special effects industry as told by the 14-year-old kid genius who grew up alongside it called Serious Creatures. Oh, and he wrote a trilogy of folk rock fantasy novels that read like Mark Twain's Dune called The Bleeding Tree Trilogy currently looking to get published.

CODY GOODFELLOW has written eight novels. His latest are UNAMERICA (King Shot Press) and SCUM OF THE EARTH (Eraserhead Press). His first two collections, SILENT WEAPONS FOR QUIET WARS and ALL-MONSTER ACTION, received the Wonderland Book Award. As an actor, he has appeared in numerous short films, TV shows, music videos and commercials. He "lives" in Portland, OR.

DAVID W BARBEE writes weird stories populated by dark monsters and strange maniacs, influenced by a deranged childhood diet of cartoons, comic books, and cult movies.

K.H. KOEHLER is a professional copyeditor and graphic designer specializing in book design and marketing. She is the author of multiple Amazon bestsellers, mostly in the pulp genre. She has over fifteen years of experience in the publishing industry as a writer, ghostwriter, copyeditor, commercial book cover designer, formatter and marketer. Visit her site at https://khkoehler.net.

LUCIO RODRIGUEZ received an MFA in creative writing from UCR's Palm Desert campus. He has stories in 18 Wheels of Science Fiction and CEA Greatest Anthology Written. His bunker is in Riverside, CA, where he hides from the dangerous outside world with his wife and two daughters. He works as an entomologist, but would never dream of combining organismal traits to create a species of slavering pack hunters.

RHYS HUGHES has lived in many countries. He currently divides his time between Britain and Kenya. In the past twenty years he has published more than forty books and nine hundred short stories, and his work has been translated into ten languages.

MAX BOOTH III was raised in Northern Indiana on an unhealthy diet of horror movies and Christopher Pike paperbacks, he now lives in San Antonio, TX where he is constantly trying not to get shot. It is harder than you think. He is the author of several novels, including Carnivorous Lunar Activities (Fangoria) and the forthcoming Touch the Night (Cemetery Dance). His non-fiction has been published online at Fangoria, LitReactor, CrimeReads, and the San Antonio Current. He is also the Editor-in-Chief of Perpetual Motion Machine, the Managing Editor of Dark Moon Digest, and the co-host of Castle Rock Radio: A Stephen King Podcast. Visit his website TalesFromTheBooth.com to learn more and follow him on Twitter @GiveMeYourTeeth.

LONNIE MILLSAP was born and raised in Los Angeles, California. Like most artists he began drawing early in life. One of his earliest artistic memeories was getting into trouble at the age of four for drawing a life sized crayon Batman on his refrigerator and grey living room carpet. Initially, he didn't get into trouble for the carpet Batman because of the way he strategically contorted his body over it. (His parents bought a new carpet a week later). While growing up Millsap drew cartoons in the borders of every paper he ever touched. His earliest artistic influences were Charles Schulz (Peanuts), Serio Argones (Mad Magazine) and Johnny Hart (Wizard of Id). As Millsap matured he was influenced by the likes of Gary Panter (Jimbo), Matt Groening (Simpsons, LIfe in Hell), Charlie Callahan and Gahan Wilson.

MIKE DUBISCH began his lifetime career in illustration and comics while still in high school, coloring comics for every major studio while writing and publishing his own short graphic works for publication. The artist never stopped exploring the subjects he enjoyed in these young years- Fantastic worlds and bizarre creatures, dynamic warriors and exotic females- and has since contributed to the worlds of Star Wars, Dungeons and Dragons, and Aliens VS Predator. His work in films and book illustration is well known by fans of the Cthulhu Mythos of H.P. Lovecraft.